Rare Bird

Gene Murray

A Wings ePress, Inc.
Mystery Novel

Wings ePress, Inc.

Edited by: Jeanne Smith
Copy Edited by: Brian Hatfield
Executive Editor: Jeanne Smith
Cover Artist: Trisha FitzGerald-Jung
Images from Pixabay

All rights reserved

Wings ePress Books
www.wingsepress.com

Copyright © 2021 by: Gene Murray
ISBN 978-1-61309-519-5
ISBN-10: 1-61309-519-8

Published In the United States Of America

Wings ePress Inc.
3000 N. Rock Road
Newton, KS 67114

Dedication

For my family, current and past, who at times drive me crazy
and yet keep me sane.

* * *

One

Never thought about it, never wanted it, never imagined my face attached to those TV heroes that solved everything in the last two minutes and then shared a joke with the sidekick as the credits rolled. But reality intrudes.

When the phone rang that day, I was inside the cage carefully removing bird droppings. I whistled softly to Lancelot and Guinevere to let them know I'd be back, and crawled out of the converted closet brushing seeds, shells, feathers, and droppings from my pants.

I was just about to say, "Thanks, I already have two of those," when I recognized Paulie's tremulous voice, sounding like each word might very well be his last. He was my oldest customer in two senses of the word: he was the oldest man I had ever worked for, and I had been doing his taxes longer than I'd been doing anyone else's. He was a short form kind of guy, but nothing else about him came easy.

"You have to help me," he wheezed. "I have no one else to turn to."

"What happened, Paulie? Don't tell me you got a letter from Internal Revenue. If they're auditing you, I'll be there with you. But your taxes are so basic they can't be—"

"No, no," he said. "It has nothing to do with taxes. It's my...I can't even talk about it over the phone. But I will say it's a very serious matter. A very serious matter. Do you think...? I know it's a lot for an old man to ask, but would you do me the kindness of coming to visit me?"

There was no need to check my calendar. It was September, and I'd been pretty much in temporary retirement since tax season ended. "Sure, Paulie. For you I can make it. I just have to clean up some. Is two o'clock okay?"

"I have an appointment with the police at two. Could you make it at one-thirty?"

"The police? Paulie, what's going on?"

"It's just that I have no one else," he whined. "Can't you please come earlier?" There are people who approach life like a Doberman Pinscher: snarling, vicious, always on the attack. Others take a less menacing route, more like a miniature French poodle. They'll straddle your leg and rub up against you until they get what they want. Paulie was a poodle. I agreed to be there by 1:30.

I rode the 7th Avenue local uptown to 86th St. and picked up a bottle of sherry for him. He lived on the fifth floor of what I think was once a fashionable hotel, but now a dilapidated apartment building inhabited mostly by senior citizens. Anyone living in the city has seen it before, or at least pictures of it...the debris, the peeling paint, the graffiti. What you don't get from the pictures are the smells and the overwhelming aura of fear and despair. There was a chain link grating covering every window on the dark staircase, and no sound but my sneakers squeaking on the steps. The elevator was still broken, had been for four years by my recollection, so I huffed and puffed my way up the five flights. I don't imagine Paulie gets out much.

He looked the same as ever, in spite of whatever was bothering him. He smiled at me, exposing huge yellow teeth that seemed to take up all of the bottom half of his skull. I never really understood the expression "long in the tooth" until I met Paulie, but he personified it. Sallow, liver-spotted skin was stretched tight over a frail skeleton, and he had only a few wispy strands of white hair left to top it off.

He had the inward sloping chest and outward sloping stomach of a man who was probably thin when he was young. When I was first introduced to him, he was around sixty and looked eighty. He was eighty now, and still looked eighty. In a few years, maybe he may start to look good for his age.

He didn't shake hands with me, just nodded pleasantly and backed into the apartment. I think I may have accidentally squeezed too hard once. But he took the sherry in his pale, bony fingers and smiled his Halloween smile.

"Oh, Arthur," he said. That's my given name, Arthur. Arthur Francis McCullough. "You're always too kind. You didn't have to bring me anything. Such a nice young man."

A lot of people say I'm nice, but at forty-three and beginning to slope a little myself, I'm not often called young anymore.

He waved me into the apartment. "Sit down, Arthur, please. Make yourself at home," he said, and disappeared into the kitchen with the sherry. I do taxes for a lot of retired people in this neighborhood, and I always try to bring a little something when I come. Danish, cookies, wine; anything to turn the angst of a tax return into something reasonably pleasant. I've probably brought twenty bottles of sherry to Paulie over the years. He always thanks me politely, but never opens the bottle and never offers me any. I wonder if he hates the stuff. For all I know, he's a recovering alcoholic and can't open them. Or maybe he's going for the *Guinness Book of World Records* in the Collection of Unopened Sherry Bottles category.

While he was shuffling around in the kitchen, cataloging the latest addition to the hoard, I looked around his living room, a clash of 1940s middle class affluence and twentieth century senior-citizen poverty. It was in semi-darkness, except where the rips in the window shades admitted long shafts of afternoon sunlight. A thin carpet, originally either gray or green, covered all but the perimeter of the hardwood floor. Spidery cracks ran along the ceiling plaster and down the wall. The furnishings, by contrast, were stately, well made and well cared for. They spoke of a life in this room that was once comfortable, decorous and social. The chair I sat in was a large, overstuffed channel back, the kind Alistair Cooke used to sit in while discussing the most recent turn of events on *Masterpiece Theatre*. Or maybe it was Alistair Cookie on *Sesame Street*. Or both.

"Good evening," I said to the dust motes. "In our last episode..."

Across the room was an armoire made of oak...classy and beautifully crafted. I had admired it before, and knew it had been made by Paulie's roommate, Walter Rupert, about 50 years ago. Rupert was a carpenter by trade, and he had been sharing this place with Paulie for twenty-five or thirty years. If you can imagine Bert and Ernie as octogenarians, you have a pretty good picture of Paulie and Walter. Paulie was the serious one, cautious, thoughtful, and a little distant. Walter was an energetic, gregarious type who liked to tell me stories of old New York, but he never let me do his taxes. I don't think he trusted me. I probably have Dad to thank for that.

Walter had a way with a story, though. He always made me feel that in the New York of the forties, life was somehow better. Cleaner. Fairer. Men were stronger, women prettier, and problems solvable. These days, you can get clubbed for thinking about men and women in prehistoric terms like strength and beauty.

Paulie came in from the kitchen, expressionless as always, hands empty as always. "Paulie," I said. "I was just thinking about Mr. Rupert. I'd like to say hello. Is he around?"

Stupid. Just a stupid question, and I realized it the moment it came out of my mouth. Inquiring about the whereabouts of an eighty-year-old man was just plain stupid. Paulie fixed a wide-eyed, horrified stare at me and lowered himself gingerly onto a creaky looking ottoman.

"Dead," he said sadly.

I was startled, as I usually am by that word. We sat quietly for a moment, avoiding each other's eyes, avoiding our own thoughts. I never know what to say at funerals or wakes, or at any mention of the 'D' word. All responses, no matter how sincere, are equally lame. 'I'm sorry' just doesn't mean anything. That's what you say when you step on someone's foot, not when a person dies. 'You have my sympathy.' Who cares? No one wants your sympathy. They want things the way they used to be. Sometimes I think that's what people want most in life. They just want things to be the way they used to be. I know I do.

The polite thing, of course, would be to ask for more information. I already knew 'who,' 'where' seemed irrelevant, and 'why' would take us into realms of existentialism better left unexplored. So, it was a choice between 'when' and 'what.'

"What happened?" I asked, cautiously.

"He was murdered right here in this apartment, last night. That's why I asked you to come." Way too complex an answer for a relatively simple question.

"Whew. I guess that also explains your appointment with the police," I said. "But I'm only your accountant, Paulie. I don't see how I can help."

He leaned forward, stared at me, and stuck out his chin. "Don't you still have that license?" he asked.

Right on cue, a little bell went off in my head, and I experienced a brief vision of the second of two shoes about to drop. Research psychologists have uncovered this phenomenon in several cases where a foolish but well-meaning man was about to become hopelessly embroiled in someone else's business.

"My investigator's license, you mean?" I do have a private investigator's license, but that fact runs squarely against type. My jaw is not what anyone would call square, and my eyes are only steely gray when my contacts have been in too long. I got the license so I could do income tax and corporate finance investigation, balance sheets, profit and loss statements, that kind of thing. It isn't real glamorous work, and I don't do very much of it, but it's real safe and it pays some bills. I get to work at home in my pajamas and, so far, no one holding a statue of a black bird has dropped dead at my feet. I'd probably throw up if someone did.

"Yes," I said hesitantly, "I still have it. But if he was murdered, then it's something for the police to handle." I could sort of feel something poodle-ish rubbing up against my leg.

"He was murdered!" Paulie said with a sudden vehemence, a flash of life in those tired, tired eyes. "He was murdered, and I want you to find out who did it."

"Paulie," I said, "murder really isn't my line of work. I just do tax fraud, embezzlement kind of stuff. Don't you think the police are better equipped—"

"The police have been here," he interrupted angrily, which surprised me. I could actually see a small vein throbbing on his forehead. "They brought their notepads and their preconceived notions. Those fools told me Walter committed suicide. Can you believe that? Walter Rupert committing suicide?" He pulled himself to his feet and began to tremble and make gulping noises.

"Slow down," I said, steering him to the couch, "and tell me what happened. Tell it from the beginning."

He took a deep breath, blew his nose twice, and told me the story. He had been awakened around three a.m. by noises from Walter's bedroom. He being slow, and it being at the far end of the hallway, it was a few minutes before Paulie could rouse himself and get to Walter's room. He found it empty and breezy, and the window leading to the fire escape was wide open.

He could see through the metal slats of the fire escape that Mr. Rupert lay, sprawled and broken, a white contrast to the dark pavement, five stories below. Paulie called to him a few times, held his breath waiting for movement, and then dialed 911.

I've given you the condensed version. Paulie's telling took about 10 minutes, and was accompanied by dramatic gestures, facial expressions and sound effects. I don't think I mentioned that Paulie was a storyteller. I don't mean he was a liar, but a professional storyteller. After his retirement from the Transit Authority, he supplemented his income by performing at street fairs, preschools, kids' birthday parties, anywhere that would hire him. When he was younger, he was pretty good at it, so I wasn't sure how much of this story was fact, and how much was craft.

"And the police choose to believe he committed suicide?" I asked.

He would have liked to rail and rant more about the police, but the long narrative had worn him out.

"Yes," he said. "But you and I know better."

"So, why then, Paulie? I know this is New York, and New Yorkers do crazy things, but why would someone kill Walter?"

Paulie slumped back on the couch and said, "It was for his book. It had to be." The buzzer rang, and he nodded to me to press the button and let him in. "That would be the new version of the Keystone Kops," Paulie said.

I opened the door to a man wearing a cream-colored poplin suit, holding a badge and ID picture and breathing hard. The man matched the picture pretty well: early thirties, a little chubby, broad smile on a cherubic face. His hair had a slight pompadour. He looked a little like Bing Crosby, if Bing Crosby were overweight and carried a gun.

"I'm Detective Chasko," he panted, with a smile that had probably been practiced before a mirror. "I believe I have an appointment with Mr. Dwyer."

I let him in and made introductions. Chasko gave me an odd look. "And can I ask who you are?"

"I'm an old acquaintance of Mr. Dwyer," I said. "I usually help him with his taxes."

His eyes narrowed. "Ever been on the police force? You look vaguely familiar."

"No, Detective. It's not the kind of work I would enjoy," I said.

Paulie's brief fire was just smoldering now, and he only nodded at Chasko's outstretched hand.

"First of all," Chasko said to Paulie, "I am truly sorry about your loss, Mr. Dwyer. I understand that Mr., uh, Rupert, was your roommate for a good number of years. You have my sympathy and that of the whole department." Smooth. Suave. Sincere. All the right words in just the right order.

"I'm sorry to burden you at a difficult time with a police interview, but our procedure is to investigate all accidents of this kind as homicides until the facts prove otherwise. Although I believe in this case the facts speak for themselves." He said all of that with the long-faced gravity of a weatherman forecasting a rainy Labor Day weekend.

"It was not an accident," Paulie muttered in our general direction. "It was not a suicide. Walter was murdered."

Chasko's smile drooped for a moment, but didn't slip off altogether. He nodded meaningfully, and carefully extracted official-looking papers from the file folder under his arm. "From the responding officer's report, there were no signs of a forced entry. We did a quick check for prints and no non-resident fingerprints were found. The coroner's report mentions no evidence of trauma before the fall. By your own report, Mr. Dwyer, there was nothing missing from the room or from the rest of the apartment. It's hard to infer murder from those circumstances."

"Walter was murdered," Paulie repeated softly.

Chasko paused, blinked and sighed deeply. "Did mister, uh… Rupert…have any enemies that you're aware of?"

Paulie looked up at him angrily. "Mister uh, Rupert, was a gentleman and well respected by everyone who knew him."

"Can you tell me anything about the gentleman's state of mind over the past few days?" A pencil and pad appeared to make it all official.

"He was very angry. For reasons you probably wouldn't understand, Walter was an unhappy, bitter man. He was angry most of the time."

"Ah, I see." The smile was gone now; the face became serious and the eyebrows pulled together for a consultation. The salesman was replaced by the psychologist. "Irrational anger can be a symptom of depression and a precursor to suicide."

Paulie pushed himself to his feet and shook a gaunt fist at the detective. "Don't you dare put words in my mouth! His anger was not irrational, and right at the moment, neither is mine. Some crazy person broke into this apartment and killed Walter Rupert, and you haven't done a blessed thing about it."

"Sir, with all due respect," Chasko said, "we have no motive for murder, no fingerprints we can't match to the residents, no indication of trauma before the fall, and nothing missing from the room. By your own admission, he had no enemies and nothing valuable enough to steal."

"What do you know about what's valuable, you pompous fraud? A man's life is valuable. His heritage is valuable."

Chasko took a deep breath and was about to launch a salvo. I stepped between them quickly before Paulie got himself arrested for assault. "You'll have to excuse Mr. Dwyer," I said. "They were very close and this has been very upsetting. He apologizes." Paulie was trembling and gulping again, which was as close to an apology as Chasko was likely to get.

He glared at me for a moment, but then downshifted a bit and went back to nodding and smiling. He rearranged his official papers and became charming again. After a long, awkward silence, Paulie said firmly, "Arthur, would you show this gentleman out of my home? He's made his position perfectly clear."

Chasko continued smiling, but with less wattage, and said to both of us, "We'll keep the file open. If any other evidence arises, or if you remember anything that could be helpful, Mr. Dwyer, please contact my office immediately."

At the door he said to me, "May I have your name, please? Just to satisfy the paperwork." He made a note on the inside of the folder. He handed me a business card, winked at me, and was gone. I haven't been winked at since I was five years old. I didn't like it then either.

"Now do you understand why I called you, Arthur? I just can't understand these people. They're children! Cops that call for appointments and leave business cards. They're just completely beyond my ken. Humphrey Bogart could whip a room full of them without breaking a sweat. I think Lauren Bacall could whip a room full of them. Pansies. Candy-asses, pardon my language. Frauds. This is why I need your help."

I got him back down on the couch and gave him a minute to catch his breath. "This isn't my line of work, Paulie. I do corporate shenanigans, tax fraud. I work with numbers. Debits and credits. Assets and liabilities. I don't know anything about murder."

He scoffed. "You probably know more than Nancy Drew over there."

"Ha. Miss Marple."

"Maxwell Not-So-Smart," he said.

We both laughed at that one, and it seemed to cheer him up a bit. "Whatever you think of his style, Paulie, he did make some good points. You really don't have any hard evidence that Walter was killed. I'll admit, he didn't seem to be the kind of person to commit suicide, but who does seem that kind? Loved ones never see it coming. And it could have been an accident."

"It wasn't an accident. For one, why would he be out there? And two, the rails out there are above my waist. He would have had to climb over the side, which he could not do with his bad hip. He was killed, and he was killed for his book."

"Right, the book you mentioned. What book are you talking about? Did Mr. Rupert write a book?"

He stared at me for a moment. My mother stared at me exactly the same way the time I threw up in church.

"No, he didn't *write* a book," Paulie explained patiently. "I'm talking about a book he owned. It was a fine old copy of, what was it? Give me a minute, oh, yes, 'Pilgrim's something or other,' 'Pilgrim's Process.' No, 'Progress.' *Pilgrim's Progress*. It had been in his family for generations."

"Oh, an antique. How much was it worth? Are you saying you think it was enough to get killed for?"

"Well, yes. At least Walter was always sure it was. For the past few weeks, he had been making calls and visiting bookstores trying to sell it, much against his principles. Oh, how he hated the thought of selling that book. It was just so important to him. It was his connection to his family and his past. I'm sure you can understand that."

Family really hadn't really been very high on my list for a few years, so I just nodded. I had forgotten that Paulie knew about my father. Rupert did. too.

"So why was he trying to sell it?"

Paulie threw his arm in a wide arc and stuck his chin out at me again. "Seriously, Arthur, look around. Be a detective. Look at how we live here! Canned soup and stale bread twice a day. I borrow the newspaper from the lady down the hall to save a buck. I'm afraid to be here in this apartment, and afraid if I leave I won't make it back. Social Security checks don't go nearly as far as they used to, Arthur, or as far as they should. That's why Walter was so angry and frustrated. The cost of living and the quality of life are moving in opposite directions, especially for old men, and no one seemed the slightest bit interested in his book."

"Okay, okay, please calm down. You're right, Paulie. I see your point."

Another minute or two of breathing through his nose. "He couldn't believe it. He thought they were all in a what-do-you-call it? A conspiracy. Trying to cheat him. Until yesterday, that is. He had an offer of five hundred dollars for it yesterday. Five hundred would have helped us a lot here. He was sure it was worth even more, though. He told me if he could hold out long enough, he could get fifty thousand for it."

I have wandered through upscale antique shops on Fifth Avenue, and window shopped at pricey art galleries, but fifty grand for a book still seemed far-fetched. "Fifty thousand, really? Fifty thousand dollars? That's a lot of book. What could make it worth so much?"

"I don't know, and I don't think Walter really knew. But he never doubted it. It was the most important thing in his life, especially after his wife died. He kept that book hidden for years and, in fact, he told me his family had kept it hidden for generations. Isn't that strange? It's a hard thing when you can't enjoy something you love."

I walked over to the armoire and rubbed my finger along the molding. Solid, professional. All the corners and fittings squared and true. Not a lot of people did work this good, certainly not in the do-it-yourself generation.

"I don't know, Paulie," I said. "The whole thing sounds a bit nutty. You're telling me Walter was killed for a book that's been hidden away for years, generations even. No one but him believes it's worth more than five hundred dollars, and even he doesn't know why it's valuable. You know I like you, and I always liked Walter, but it just doesn't make a lot of sense."

He slumped, head on his chest. "Isn't that what detectives do?" he asked. "Make sense of things that don't make sense? He was killed, Arthur. I know he was. Walter was a good man and he was murdered in cold blood. Help me. Please help me."

That damn poodle had a grip on my leg again. "I can't say yes, Paulie, but I'm not going to say no. Yet. I'll do what I can, which may not be much, at least until I'm convinced the cops are right. I'm afraid that will have to be good enough."

He was not happy, but nodded and snorted his resignation. "You'll see I'm right. I know you will."

I got stuck in the middle of the Holland Tunnel one time. Summertime too, just my luck. An accident somewhere ahead of me blocked traffic in both directions until they managed to tow it out. I couldn't move forward, I couldn't move back, and I couldn't breathe very well. I was getting the same feeling talking to Paulie.

"I guess we'd better go look in his room then," I said without enthusiasm. "You know, the scene of the crime."

Two

There is a feeling you get when you walk into a place you know you shouldn't be, and don't really want to be. A house of horrors quiver. There is a subtle but fundamental shift in your reality...a psychological click, and suddenly the lower parts of your brain are in charge of your life. Your mind sweeps away all non-essential thoughts. You see, feel, and hear everything magnified as if on a giant movie screen with theater-quality stereo and a good set of earphones. There is no separation between you and your environment. There's no adjustment, just a pure Zen moment of consciousness. You have just entered another dimension, not of sight or sound, but of mind. You have just entered into...

My first crime scene. I walked carefully into the room, adrenals at warp nine, pupils dilated, hair cells upright and quivering. There was nothing overtly dramatic about it, no yellow tape to seal the room off, no chalk drawing of a fractured body on the floor. Just a drab and dusty room where an old man used to live. The bedroom had the same shabby contrast as the rest of the apartment, fine crafted furniture surrounded by dilapidation and neglect. The room was large enough to accommodate a roll-top desk, a nightstand, a dresser, and a bookshelf doing double duty as a headboard. All, I assumed, crafted by Walter in his salad days. Knickknacks, loose change, a leathery blue pouch, crumpled receipts, keys, and pictures were tossed carelessly on the desk. I looked around carefully, but only one thing seemed out of place. The dresser was pulled away from the wall and turned, as if someone had been looking back there. Nothing else looked like a clue.

"Did Walter keep the dresser pulled away like that for some reason?"

"I really don't know, Arthur. I haven't been in this room, except last night, for several months. We're both private people, like two ships stumbling past each other in the night. There were many days when I only saw him at meals, sometimes not even then. But I doubt if Walter left it like that. Why would he? Maybe the police? They were poking around in here for a good while, pretending to work."

"Yeah, probably." I climbed out onto the fire escape and Paulie pointed to where he had seen Walter's body last night. Paulie was right. The railing was almost chest high. It would have been difficult for Walter to get over it, even if he did want to commit suicide.

Paulie relaxed on the bed and called over. "You saw Walter last time you were here, right? When you did my taxes. When was that, February? March? He was using a cane then, I think. One bad hip, two bad knees, sciatica. I don't think he could have gotten over that rail."

"Yeah," I said. "It would have been a struggle just to climb through the window." I was looking down on a small courtyard formed by the backs of four buildings. The buildings were all made of brick, the fire escapes of steel and the sidewalk of cement. There wasn't a tree or a blade of grass or a squirrel to be seen. Not a very forgiving environment. I leaned over the rail a little and saw that the bottom section of ladder was about 10 or 12 feet off the ground. But there was a dumpster a few feet away that someone, someone athletic, could have used to jump to the ladder. It seemed like a stretch, but it was all I had.

"How do you think whoever it was got in? That's one of the big issues for the cops."

"I guess Walter must have left the window open a little. It's been kind of warm," Paulie said.

"Did he usually leave it open? Seems a little risky to me, even this high up."

Paulie looked sheepishly at me. He gulped, sort of shrugged, but didn't answer. Why would someone who had lived in New York City all of his life be foolish enough to leave a window open? Especially one right next to a fire escape.

I climbed back in and looked carefully around the window frame but couldn't find a sign that anything had been broken or forced. The window moved freely up and down and had a clasp that locked it. No screen or storm window. But on the bottom window frame, dead center, on the outside, was a piece of lined yellow paper taped to the glass. It was just a corner piece, blank, and could have belonged to some long-ago Christmas decoration, love note or welcome home sign. I thought it might be a piece of a legal pad. I looked at it carefully, like a detective, and could see the tape was not brown and curled with age. If it was a reminder or decoration, why was it on the outside?

Paulie padded up behind me and watched over my shoulder. "Something?" he asked, hopefully.

I just shook my head. "Tell me again," I said. "What exactly did you see and hear?"

He found his way back to the bed and sat down. He leaned back against the headboard, folded his hands across his belly and looked up at the ceiling, the position for a yarn.

"Okay, I'll go through it again for you. It's late, like three or three-thirty in the morning. I'm in bed, but awake. I usually only sleep for an hour or two, and then lie awake for a while and then sleep for another hour or two. An old man's curse. So I'm dozing and listening to the traffic outside, trying to decide if I should listen to the radio for a while. I can sometimes pick up a late-night evangelist trying to convince me that sending him money will save my soul. If I send twice as much, I can save the soul of a friend, too. I had my window open a little, too, but it doesn't have a fire escape. Then I hear voices, first muffled and not too loud, but I think they may be out in the street, or maybe in the hallway. I hope they're out in the hallway and I hope they don't mean trouble. It's quiet for a few minutes, but then I hear Walter's voice, shouting. I am sure it's his voice, but I can't really tell what the words are. It was either 'get away from there' or 'I don't care.' See, I don't sleep with my hearing aid in. But I'm scared, thinking 'something is wrong with Walter,' so I decide to investigate."

Here, Paulie pantomimed standing up, stretching, putting on a bathrobe and slippers, and shuffling down the hall. "Bathrobe, slippers and teeth just in case, and I'm just out the bedroom door when I hear a quick, sharp sound, like a slap. I think maybe whoever it was hit Walter."

"Are you sure about the slap?"

He shook his head. "No, I'm not completely sure, I didn't take the time for my hearing aid. But I'm pretty sure."

"The detective said they didn't find any extra marks on Walter's body."

"Of course he would say that. But how could they find anything after that terrible fall?"

"Another miracle of medical science, I suppose," I said.

He gave the tiniest shake of his head. "The miracle is that people still believe in science. Or medicine."

He sat up. "Or, or...maybe it's not too crazy to think Walter hit the guy."

"Yes," I said. "Knowing Walter, that's not too crazy. So what happened next?"

He assumed the position again. "I heard more noises I couldn't recognize when I got close to Walter's room, like grunting or scuffling. Like maybe there was a fight. I heard some mumbling, and then a shout. I think the voice, not Walter's voice, said, 'Tell me where it is.' I know that's what he said. That really scared me because it was so clear, so I called out, 'I've already called the police. They're on the way.' And then...I have to trust in your *total discretion*, Arthur. Something else happened here that I haven't told the police."

"I'm sorry, what? You lied to the police?"

"No, no. You know me better than that. I wouldn't lie. I just didn't mention one little thing I heard."

"Jesus, Paulie. Really, Jesus."

He was sitting up now, eyes bright, hands clasped together. I was right in front of him looking down into those sad, tired eyes, "I was scared," he said. "I'm still scared they'll think I had something to do with all of this. Like I was involved. And you know how the police can be. You, more than most people, know how the police can be."

"So what did you hear?"

"After I said that about the police, a voice shouted back, 'If you come in here, he's dead! And if you call the cops, he's dead! Just shut up and go back to bed, Paulie'."

"Jesus, Paulie," I said again. "A man's voice, right? And he called you by name?"

"Yes, and I didn't even react to that at the time. And then I heard Walter say, but soft and kind of choking, 'His name! How do you know his name?' It was all raspy and I think he might have been choking Walter. I was afraid to go in. The only thing I could think to do was to unlock the door to let the cops in. I was too afraid to even use the phone to call them, so I just sat in the living room for a few minutes, feeling feeble and stupid and cowardly. I could hear some more noises, but couldn't tell what they were. Just grunting and scraping, I think. By the time I got the courage to come in here, the room was empty, and Walter was down there. On the sidewalk."

"You didn't see anyone? Or hear anything?"

"I poked my head out the window, but I didn't think I could make it onto the fire escape by myself. Anyway, I didn't see anyone. Just Walter, on the pavement. I didn't even think it was him at first. I just couldn't believe it."

"Do you think Walter gave the guy the book?"

"Wow, um, I really don't...no. I don't think Walter would do that. It was too important to him. And besides, I don't think he had the time. It all happened so fast."

Fast is a relative term, especially when you're eighty. If any of this were true, the guy had time to climb in the window, threaten Mr. Rupert, drag him to the fire escape, and hoist him over.

"What could be so special about the book?"

"The book? Oh, I don't know. I've never known. Walter was very secretive about it."

"Where did he keep it?"

His shoulders pulled themselves up to his ears. "The book? I don't know that, either. Honestly, Arthur, I've never known. Walter always kept it hidden, even from me."

"You have seen it, haven't you?" I asked.

"Of course I've seen it. Many times. Walter would take it out once or twice a year and admire it, show it off a little, but he was always very closemouthed about where he kept it. He said, 'There's an old German proverb that three people can keep a secret, but only if two of them are dead'."

He smiled, "Just to get his goat, I would tell him that was an Irish proverb." Bert and Ernie.

So we were searching for a book that may or may not have been valuable, may or may not have been the motive for a murder, and was located in this room, in the killer's possession, or somewhere else on the planet earth. Clear as mud.

I pointed to the bookshelf. "I guess the next thing to do is search the room for the book. You don't have any idea at all where it might be, right?"

Paulie just shrugged and set to work. He pulled up a folding chair close to the bed and started going through the books in the headboard/bookshelf, one at a time. I started at the opposite side and did the same.

After half an hour of leafing and separating, we had six piles: a big stack of Civil War books, a few miscellaneous paperbacks, a lot of manuals on woodworking, a couple of short story collections by Edgar Allan Poe, books about German culture in the U.S., and a two-volume set of Whitman's *Leaves of Grass*. The one book that seemed out of place was the Betty Crocker cookbook I found on the night table.

"I thought you did all the cooking around here," I asked, flipping through the cookbook.

"I do," Paulie said. "Well, most of it, anyway. But I have my bad days, too, and sometimes Walter was good enough, and hungry enough, to pitch in."

I held up the book. "Was he planning a special meal? Most people keep their cookbooks in the kitchen."

"Walter wasn't the kind to plan a meal. He just put in a little of this and a little of that, and when it was hot, we ate it. I've never seen that book before." Inside the front cover, there was an inscription:

God gives us light,
The clouds give us rain,
I'm giving you this book
So you won't give me ptomaine

'To Angela, with love from Frank. December 1981.'

There was also a small sticker on the inside cover which read:
Grove St. Bookstore
Est. 1931
and $1.50 in small cramped handwriting.

I tossed the cookbook back onto the dresser. "You knew him better than anyone else. Where do you think he would have been hiding it?"

He sighed heavily and sat on the bed, not moving or speaking for a minute. Then he leaned over and started knocking on the headboard. "Walter made this. And he could be, you know, what's that word parallel, para...something?"

"Paranoid?"

"Yes, that. Suspicious. He could easily have built a secret compartment into this headboard."

I started tapping too, and feeling carefully around the shelves. I felt pretty stupid, like Nancy Drew herself, and was just about to give up when Paulie cried, "Ha! There it is! I knew it! I knew it!"

"The book?"

"No, no, not the book, but a little hidey-hole he built into this bookcase."

"I don't believe it," I said. "A secret compartment."

Paulie said, "If you knew Walter Rupert better, you'd believe it."

The top of the bookshelf was a double shelf hidden behind a wide, ornate molding. There was a space of about three inches between the shelves, and a small door, about six inches square, popped open from the lower shelf. Inside was a small, spiral bound notebook and seven business cards from book dealers, including Grove St. Bookstore, Est. 1931. The notebook was a diary of sorts, going back almost fifteen years in what Paulie recognized as Walter Rupert's handwriting.

I poked around until I found an identical compartment on the opposite side of the headboard, but all it had in it was a note with the famous drawing, Kilroy Was Here! It's not that Mr. Rupert had such a well-developed sense of humor; he just liked to tick people off.

"The *Pilgrim's Progress* would fit nicely in there. It's just the right size," Paulie muttered.

I scanned the first few entries of the diary quickly and said, "I'd like to get this copied, if you don't mind, so we can both look at it and compare notes."

"Are you sure that's necessary? It might be a very private diary. Maybe I should just read it and tell you what it says."

"Paulie, even if it is private, I have to know about it. I have to know a lot about Mr. Rupert, warts and all, as well as about his book, if you want me to figure this out."

He agreed, reluctantly, and I said I would get it copied and bring the original back tomorrow. As we left the room, Paulie closed the door reverently behind us. "I feel so terrible about what happened, and I feel it might have been my fault," he said.

"Your fault? How?"

"If I hadn't yelled about the police, maybe that goon wouldn't have killed Walter. Maybe he would have just robbed the place and left us alone. Or maybe if I had called the cops earlier. Or maybe if I had a pistol. Walter always wanted us to get a pistol, but I was against it."

"I don't know about that, Paulie," I said. "If whoever it was really came with a purpose, there was nothing you could have done. You're lucky you did say that, or you might have been hurt, too. If you had just walked in here, no telling what could have happened."

"Yeah, maybe. Maybe I did the right thing."

"It's interesting, though, that you heard a slap, but the police found no marks on the body...well, maybe it was the long fall."

"But I feel like I should have done something more. I feel like I abandoned Walter."

I thought of some more questions a good detective should ask, mostly to get him thinking about something else.

"Who else knew about the book?" I asked.

"As far as I'm aware, only me. Oh, maybe a neighbor, but she couldn't be involved."

"Did Mr. Rupert have any family left?"

"He has a daughter, a lovely girl she was, but they were estranged. I don't think Walter has seen Marguerite in twenty or twenty-five years. Hasn't talked about her, either."

"So if it turns out that this book is valuable, who gets it?"

"Well, Walter was kind enough to include me in his will."

"What did he leave you?" I asked.

"Well," he said sheepishly. "Actually, everything he owned," he said in a voice that sounded just a little stronger, just a little younger than the Paulie I knew.

Three

Subway.

The British call their system "the underground," which hints at a somewhat more romantic method of travel. *Le Metro,* the French version, sounds old world and sophisticated. "Trolley" brings a totally different image to bear. My mind's eye conjures a smiling conductor, complete with pot belly, handlebar mustache, and starched blue uniform. He operates his machine cheerfully and occasionally turns to smile at the passengers happily rocking, bouncing, and smiling right back at him.

But New York has just 'the subway,' a relatively cheap, relatively quick, and entirely disagreeable method of transportation. At the best of times, it's dirty, smelly, noisy, and dangerous. At rush hour, which is actually about two and a half hours long, it becomes dirtier, smellier, noisier, and even more dangerous. Those unfortunates who ride it every day, *Les Misérables*, are transformed from Homo sapiens, the zenith of evolutionary development, into nameless and wretched packages of skin, bones and brain, with few rights and no dignity. Rainy days are special, when complete strangers have the opportunity to drip all over you, but hot, summer days are the biggest challenge, when six hundred square feet of late afternoon humanity surrounds you. There seems to be no limit to what people will suffer just to get to work on time. Rush hour. Been there, done that, and not doing it again.

It was just before four o'clock, and the stations were empty and quiet...the calm before the storm. There was a guy—it may have been a guy—curled up and asleep—he may have been asleep—at the far end of the station. At this time of day, the token vendors are busy reading the *New York Post* and dreaming up new ways to be surly. The muggers are home sharpening their knives and trying pantyhose on their heads. The pickpockets are in their studio apartments doing finger flex exercises. And the horde, the ones leading lives of quiet desperation, are still at work being desperately quiet.

I walked from Paulie's apartment to 86th Street because there was a big express station there. Some people do their best thinking in the shower, some just before they fall asleep, and some sitting at a bar staring at a row of bottles. I do some of my best thinking in an empty subway station. It has a cathedral-like atmosphere of vast, high-vaulted hugeness, and the compressed silence of a calm ocean or the Grand Canyon. Also, thinking about something else helps me forget I'm in the subway.

I thought about Jonesy...my paramour, inamorata, main squeeze. Jonesy is a freelance photographer, with an accent on the 'free.' In the six years I've known her, I don't think she's sold a single picture. I don't actually think she's tried to. She's in it, she says, for the art, not the commerce. Currently, there are photographs all over her apartment. Her favorite is one of a pear-shaped midget caught in the translucent reflection of a pear-shaped window of a pear-shaped jewelry store, aptly titled 'Appearances.'

"It's baroque," she told me one time.

"Someone should fix it," I muttered when I knew she couldn't hear.

Her most recent opus is a pear montage of New York's architectural landmarks. The Guggenheim Museum, the Empire State Building, the Statue of Liberty, the Flatiron Building, St. Patrick's Cathedral, Gracie

Mansion...all skillfully blended together in her darkroom and set on a bright yellow background. It looked to me like a bowl of pears with points and windows, but I have always been careful not to say so. All this is characteristic, I think, of art and not money.

Who am I kidding? It's a little too much to say I worship the ground she walks on, but she tramps all over the ground I worship. She has a passion for her art, for her life, that I have never been able to muster. She does most things thoughtlessly, but with grace and poise, and she is never caught off guard. I am careful not to use the word 'love' with her, because that would probably scare her off, but also because I'm not sure what I feel for her is love. Not traditional love, anyway. It's a couple of local stops past admiration, and one or two stops before awe.

Soon after completing the landmarks program, she began to feel she had 'done' New York. A few Loretta Lynn tapes and a Georgia O'Keeffe book later, she decided she was 'raised on country sunshine,' or some damn thing, and made plans to move to Montana. Or is it Wisconsin? West of Jersey City I get all confused. I do know that the Dodgers moved to L.A. in 1956, and in more or less rapid succession the Giants moved to San Francisco, Johnny Carson moved to Burbank, and the Jets and football Giants slipped across the river to New Jersey. I may be new to the detective game, but I know a dangerous trend when I see one.

What Jonesy needs, she says, is the psychic inspiration of new material. She's tired of transforming architecture into fruit. She wants to photograph the nobly weathered faces of America's farmers, truck drivers, and cattle rustlers. Maybe she'll get a bunch of pear-shaped farmers together and make them look like the New York skyline. Now that would be truly baroque.

Jonesy Shaw is her real name, by the way. Chosen by her mother and duly recorded on all official documents. She told me that she once asked her mother, a frequently married woman of dependent means, how she came to pick the name Jonesy.

"I really can't remember, dear," her mother had answered as she dabbed some sample perfume on her wrist. "Do you think this will clash with my new chinchilla hat?" Maybe I made that up, but it's in sync with her general approach to life in the 80s.

A train rumbled into the station, interrupting my thoughts, and I settled into a seat across from a middle-aged, overweight woman with a ring through her eyebrow and a pink streak in her hair. She had an infant in a carrier next to her, and kept her quiet by refilling her bottle with root beer. It's commonly known that early nutrition is a prerequisite for success in life.

As the local stations whizzed by, I wondered when, actually if, Jonesy was going to ask me to go to Montana with her, and I wondered what I would say. In spite of the universal appeal of cow pies and ten-gallon hats, the whole enterprise didn't make sense. I didn't think she really wanted to go.

She showed up for dinner that night carrying, as usual, her dry cleaning. For her, dry cleaning was a symbol of status worn proudly over her arm, her see-through badge of courage. Even now when I think of her, I see a thin, angular woman with perfectly cut hair, sauntering regally down a crowded street with a plastic bag full of clothes over her arm.

She had an odd way of greeting me...almost a hug, and almost a pat on the back. She would throw one arm, whichever wasn't carrying dry cleaning, around my neck and pat me on the back, but very softly. Sometimes a kiss on the cheek, sometimes she would just pull quickly away. She was dressed casually today: jeans, sweatshirt and a baseball cap without a logo. "I won't advertise for anyone without being paid," she explained one time. She draped the dry cleaning carefully over a chair and told me she had spent the morning photographing a jail in The Bronx from 63 angles, and spent the afternoon shopping. There's a surprise.

"And, oh!" she said excitedly, "I picked up my tickets from the travel agent today. I'm flying out on Thursday next."

"But I thought you weren't leaving until after Thanksgiving."

"Well, I'm not moving until then, but I'm going to spend a week or two in Billings to get set up. Find an apartment and a bank and deal with all that practical stuff."

"Billings," I said. "Billings."

"Don't do that tonight, Bird. Don't go all Woody Allen on me."

I stirred my sambuca, careful not to look at her. "Have you really thought this through?" I asked, as quietly, levelly, as I could manage. "You don't know anything about living in the country. Do you know what's in Wisconsin? Wild animals. And snakes. Domestic terrorists and FBI agents. And cowboys and blizzards and drought and, if all that wasn't bad enough, country music! Country music all up and down the AM dial, because there is no FM dial. No jazz, no public radio, just dust and pickup trucks and rifles. Everybody out there has a rifle. And big hats and belt buckles. And cheese."

"Bird," she said calmly. "Wisconsin has cheese. I'm going to Montana."

"Montana's even worse," I said. "They don't even have cheese there. Or cold cuts. And it's a day's drive to an all-night deli."

"*Annie Hall*, right? You're channeling Alvy, and we're doing *Annie Hall* again."

"Oh, come on Jonesy. We've had this conversation before. It's just that there is, really is, a fundamental, intrinsic difference between West and East. Them and us. It's a cultural thing."

"Okay," she said. "I'm up for a little *Trivial Pursuit*. We did Alvy Singer and Annie Hall. Oh, here's one. Alan Alda and Jane Fonda in *California Suite*. He wants the easy life in L.A., she wants the challenge and grit of New York."

I thought for a moment. "Don't forget John Belushi and I don't remember who else in *Continental Divide*. He wanted to live in the East, she wanted him to move out West."

"Two points for the boys' team. Anyone else?"

"Uh, let me see. Neil Diamond singing to himself on 'I Am...I Said.' What ho, Watson! We've stumbled onto a commonplace, cultural, bi-coastal, conundrum. Whatever can the answer be?"

She thought for a moment and then started counting the casualties on her fingers. "Woody and Diane Keaton broke up, and each had fabulously successful solo careers. Alan and Jane parted the best of friends and stayed on separate coasts and both had fabulously successful solo careers. Belushi and whoever, got married and lived in Chicago, more or less the midpoint, but then he overdosed and died, ruining a fabulously successful career. Neil Diamond moved to L.A., turned gray at the temples and started turning out fabulously derivative, but successful, trash."

"Which leaves us where?" I asked, feeling a little uncomfortable about the term 'solo career.'

She was quiet, knowing that silence was her best move, always. As long as words were being exchanged, there was still a chance for me to score, win the point, snatch victory from the jaws of defeat. But when she was quiet, looking at me or not, next to me or on the other side of the room, I was lost. The azure eyes, the patrician nose, the Audrey Hepburn chin and sleek, swan-curving neck, sloped to conquer. Once again, she was trampling the ground I worship.

With the slightest of movements, she looked over at me and said, "Bird." That's all. That's all she ever had to say. Just "Bird." End of discussion. The fat lady has sung, sprayed her tonsils, had dinner, said her prayers and gone to bed. I can only sigh.

Jonesy took off her shoes and swung her feet over my legs. "So, what did you do today? You didn't work on the wall, it's not dusty enough in here."

"I went over to see Paulie Dwyer. Did I ever tell you about him?"

"One of the old guys uptown. Tells you long stories."

"That's him, and he told me a pip today. His roommate was killed in a burglary, and he wants me to investigate."

She bit down on the ice from her drink. "You? Does he think you're some kind of a cop?"

"Actually, I am some kind of a cop." I made the mistake once of bragging to her that I had a private investigator's license. One of the reasons I went through the trouble of getting the damn thing was to impress her. A complete waste of time. On my good days, I'm sure she loves me, but more and more, I don't have good days. It took me a while to realize that nothing I did ever impressed her. Like most men who are with an attractive woman, I didn't understand what she saw in me. I have as much muscle tone as licorice, and I'm too tall, which makes me hunch over a bit. I have thin hair, a beak for a nose, small eyes and hardly any eyebrows. On the other hand, I don't drink much, take drugs or sleep around. I don't work too much or watch too much TV. I seem to be at a point in life when my assets and liabilities more or less balance each other.

I told her the story of Mr. Rupert and the book, or the alleged book.

"Sounds like a real mystery," she said. "Think you're detective enough to handle it?"

"I told Paulie I would do what I can, but the whole deal sounds like something from a *Law and Order* rerun. Anyway, I'm not sure I'm going to be around long enough to find out."

"Not around long enough?" she said with a half-smile.

"No, I may be in Wisconsin holding your camera bag."

She smiled and turned off the light behind her, leaned toward me and said, "Not Wisconsin, Bird. Montana."

"Whatever," I said, slipping my hand between her ankles. "Wherever. But I still don't get it."

She pulled away and sat up straight. She breathed a long, slow, deep sigh. "You know very well we're not the people we were six years ago, Bird," she said to her drink. That sounded like it was leading somewhere I didn't want to go, so I said nothing.

"When I met you," she continued, "you were the most confused and frightened person I'd ever seen. You were terrified. You were actually afraid to leave your loft."

"Yes, and thanks so much for reminding me."

"I'm not trying to hurt you. I'm trying to explain."

"I was in trouble then. I had people with cameras and microphones camping at my front door. *Banging* on my front door. What does that have to do with you moving to Wisconsin?"

"Do you remember how we met?" She was still now, cobra still. Staring into my eyes like it was a grip. And it was.

"Of course. You surprised me inside a *Chock Full o' Nuts*. You asked if you could take my picture. I never did find out how you found me there."

"I didn't *find* you. I wasn't looking for the 'Loft Lizard.' I was just looking for an interesting face to photograph. I think I was into faces that winter."

"You were shivering. I bought you coffee and asked you to take it somewhere else. So, of course, you sat down and ate half of my English muffin."

"Yeah. And you were totally spooked. You thought I was gonna blow a whistle and summon a hundred reporters. Bird, I didn't know anything about you, or your father. I had never heard that stupid term,'Loft Lizard,' either. I just wanted a face, and yours was the best one available."

"It was the first time I had been out of the loft in about three days and I was hungry. I had to go up on the roof and cross to another building to get away from the horde. Those people are rabid when they get a scent."

"Yeah, well, I don't care about all that. I didn't then and I don't now. I was kind of crosswise with one of my stepfathers. A little angry and a lot lost. You were good for me, and I was good for you, but I'm not sure we're good for each other anymore."

"Yes, we were good together. We could be again. Even in Wisconsin, if I had to."

"That's not the point, and you know it."

"Then what? I want to be with you. You are, at least, comfortable with me. What's wrong with that?"

"Montana. I'm moving to Montana, and I'm trying to explain." She took a deep breath. "You needed me then, you don't anymore. There, I said it."

"You're a woman of the twentieth century. You don't define yourself by what other people need."

"Oh, crap. I don't put myself in any era, and I don't bother to define myself at all. I'm past all of that. My consciousness has been raised about as far as it can go, and I need to make some changes in my life."

"So, Montana?"

"Yes, Montana. Why not? As good a place as any."

I lay back on the couch and balanced my drink on my chest, still waiting for her to ask me to go with her. Through the half-closed blinds, I could see the top layer of one small corner of my city in semi-darkness. A block of white lights here, a red blinker there, lit up in a futile attempt to avoid tragedy. Beyond the lights it was pitch black, just the way it was meant to be.

Man struggles to conquer and control the world around him. He levels it, builds on it, and thinks he has made it useful and safe and tame. But it's too big, too complicated, too indifferent to our digging and decorating. The guy who scrambles to the top has the farthest to fall. Never stand next to a man who's got it all, because a safe is about to land on his head.

Dinner was quiet, with minimal eye contact, and conversation only about the weather and the Yankees. She didn't ask me to go to Montana, and I didn't volunteer. It wasn't exactly a final curtain. It was hanging on to a thread wrapped around my pinky while my pants were falling off. Yogi said, 'It ain't over till it's over,' but when Mazeroski hit that home run, it was definitely over. So, what did he know?

After she left, I finished the bottle of sambuca and managed to resist opening another.

~ * ~

I only seem to dream just before I wake up, and usually I can only remember snippets of it. That night perhaps the sambuca helped, but I had a clear memory of something, but only something brief. I am looking down at the floor of a political convention where thousands of people are holding up masks of their favorite candidate. Thousands of little cardboard faces attached to Popsicle sticks bob up and down in time to the tune of "Happy Days Are Here Again." And each one of them is the face of my father.

His, ours I guess, was the scandal *du jour* during last year's scandal monsoon season. Unfortunately for me, it was local, focused on only a few villains, and the press was looking for something to do.

Dad, William J. McCullough, always used the most basic and elegant of business cards...just his name in bold, and underneath it the word 'Entrepreneur.' That summed him up pretty well. A jack of all trades, master of nothing he was willing to talk about, and willing to do anything if the risk was small and the payoff was big. Small, athletic, fastidious and bright, he is in many ways my opposite. He has a great heart, great appetites, and no scruples.

He and his partner owned a few strip malls in Queens and Brooklyn, developed out of seed money from the partner's family. I used to call him Uncle Allan, but now that he is in jail, I don't call him anything at all.

The money from the sale was about three times the value of the property, and that raised some alarms at the time that something, probably in the realm of money laundering, was involved. The alarms were quickly swaddled in the good fellowship of friends in high places and Dad's only problem became finding something legal to do with the money.

The answer had come from Uncle Allan. "Buy your son a loft in Manhattan, and in two years you will triple your money. Or his money, depending on how you 'gift' it." That was the first time I had ever heard 'gift' used as a verb, and some distant alarm bells went off for me as well. But that may be just 20/20 hindsight.

I moved my three rooms of furniture into this loft, big enough to be a roller rink, and began to rehab it. Within a year, the whole scheme started to unravel. Dad, who made very few mistakes, made a big one then. He applied for a position as operations liaison for the speaker of the city council. The job would be right where the money changed hands, but he thought it was deep enough in the maze of government functionaries that he would be invisible.

Got that one wrong, Dad.

An exposé by the *Long Island Press* uncovered what were called 'financial irregularities' in the sale of those Brooklyn strip malls. But there was no follow-up, for whatever reason, until a few weeks later when a small paper from White Plains picked up the threads and started to sew them into a narrative. Kickbacks, money laundering, just a hint of extortion, and the game was on.

Denials, followed by finger-pointing, followed by subpoenas, followed by trials. I had very little to do in the melee, only a couple of depositions by a squadron of hostile city attorneys. But it was clear I was only an end, never a means. Eventually, after a few months of hounding, even the press painted me as an ingenue in this opera. The news cycle shifted after the college basketball finals and Chernobyl, and they left me alone. Mostly. Occasionally, I come across someone like Chasko, who wants to open old wounds. Other than that, I don't think about my father. I don't worry about him. At least not when I'm awake.

~ * ~

I awoke to a beautiful morning, one of those crisp, fall mornings that makes you miss summer and dread winter. A deep blue-sky morning with only the faintest wisps of white clouds. The bright sun was complemented by a steady cooling breeze, the way cheesecake goes with a good cup of coffee. It was a day for kites and poets, not old books and sudden, violent death.

I, by contrast, felt as empty and abandoned as the Jersey shore in November. Absolutely nothing worked for me that morning. I showered and still felt dirty, shaved and still felt stubbly, dressed and still felt naked. My cereal tasted like cardboard, and the coffee tasted like cereal.

I put my feet up on the sill of the western window, my hand wrapped around my favorite seagull mug, and watched my small piece of the Hudson River between the buildings. I was born in Manhattan, have lived here my whole life and never really wanted to live anywhere else. I don't think many people can say that. In fact, statistics show almost no one ever does say that. For years after my father's implosion, it was a dark city, filled with alien and scary people and threatening things, until Jonesy showed me the beauty hiding in the dark, and how to find light when I needed it. Which would be more unbearable, I wondered, Jonesy without the city or the city without Jonesy? There's just no telling what kind of sludge will seep into conscious thought when you've had too much sambuca. After a second cup of cornflakes, I laced up my running shoes and headed uptown to the information super rest stop.

The beauty of the 42nd Street library, like many other New York City attractions, requires a special visual trick, a perceptual screening, to be truly appreciated. You have to see the building itself while ignoring the lunch bags, beer cans and newspapers that our citizens feel is their right, nay duty, to deposit on those celebrated steps. As I walked between Patience and Fortitude, the stone lions guarding the entrance, I passed a young man with his hands deep in the pockets of his camo jacket.

"Smoke, coke, ups, and downs. All good stuff. Check it out." I had been foolish enough to smoke a joint or two in my salad days, but I thought people stopped doing that stuff years ago.

Inside the library, I found a few general works on book collecting and settled myself into a chair to read. After a lot of chatter about how much fun collecting books can be, and how you really don't need a lot of money to have a fine book collection (you can even collect books on book collecting), I skipped to the chapter entitled, 'What Makes a Book Valuable.'

It seems there aren't many rules, and the ones that exist allow for so many exceptions they barely qualify as rules. Age, in and of itself, has little bearing on the value of a book. However, combined with other factors, it can make a world of difference.

First editions are usually more valuable than second or subsequent editions. And the smaller the number published in the edition, the more valuable it may someday become.

Books that have been inscribed by famous authors, or owned by famous people and autographed to prove it, take on additional value.

Old books in good condition are more valuable than old books in not so good condition. Not hard to believe that one.

Finally, the only rule that applies to all books at all times is the Economics 101 standby, supply and demand. A book is valuable if another person wants to buy it, and its value is determined exclusively by how much the other person is willing to pay for it. In the hyperdrive Manhattan of the eighties, that leaves a lot of room for mayhem.

I then found a copy of *Pilgrim's Progress* with an extensive forward explaining the history and meaning of the book. It was first published in 1678, and is one of the most frequently published books in English literature. Basically a religious tract, it deals with heaven and hell, righteousness and wickedness, good and evil, black and white, winners and losers, them against us, on and off, ones and zeros, yin versus yang. The type of thing so prevalent in fiction and so absent in fact. Who says life imitates art?

I waded through about fifteen pages of the adventures of Christian, Obstinate, Evangelist, etc., as they make their way from the City of Destruction through Vanity Fair and the Valley of the Shadow of Death, toward the Celestial City. Fifteen pages was more than enough to get the general gist, and to make my eyes start to roll back in my head, so I decided to try the trade periodicals. There were several dealing directly with book collecting, and I knew the bulk of my day's work would be plodding through these magazines trying to learn if, and why, Mr. Rupert's book could be valuable.

There were several reference works available: *American Book Collector*, *Antiquarian Bookman*, and *The Bibliognost* (for those who believe the existence of books can never be known by man). They were all factual, informative and as boring as a typing class. I looked carefully through the first few issues and flipped through the next several, but found no reference to *Pilgrim's Progress*. They did have a lot of other wildly popular items listed, like *British Diving Ducks*, *Italian Doorways*, and *Historic Notices in Reference to Fatheringay*. Wow.

All of this was terribly interesting, but offered no clue as to why a book hidden by a family for at least three generations could suddenly be worth a large sum of money. I now knew a little about book collecting, but I still knew nothing about Mr. Rupert's book. For all I knew, it was the first copy of *Pilgrim's Progress* ever printed. For all I cared, it could have been the last. Judging by the fifteen pages I read, it should have been banned by some mental health organization centuries ago.

It could have been owned by John Bunyan himself, who willed it to his gigantic, bucolic son Paul. While in the hands of Paul Bunyan in the pristine forests of pre-industrial America, it was involved in some wonderful adventures, including the fatal crash of Casey Jones... maybe Casey was reading it at the time. It could easily have been the book that put Rip Van Winkle to sleep for twenty years, but what did it have to do with the death of Walter Rupert? I forced myself to page through issues as much as two years back, uncertain about what I was looking for and not really understanding what I was looking at.

That proved fruitless, so I spent the next fifteen minutes feeding dimes into a machine to copy Mr. Rupert's notebook, and then walked back home. I didn't feel like thinking about old books or girlfriends or murder. I wanted to think about my home. A lot of stuff you read talks about two New Yorks: the old and the new, or the rich and the poor. Sometime it's the three New Yorks: business, arts and residential. Or the four New Yorks or five boroughs or six walking tours or seven socioeconomic groups. All of these number games miss the point. New York is too deep, too busy, too complicated to be put in any neat little package. It's an ocean, teeming with life and the remains of previous life, where the waves swell, peak, and crash, and the elements are absorbed and reconstituted to do it all over again. A person of the seventh socioeconomic group on walking tour number two in the residential section of the third borough can think himself firmly planted in that time, space and dimension. But blink once and turn around, and everything is different. A slight change in perspective creates a whole new reality around you, and all you have to do is see it. It's like one of those *Family Circus* cartoons where one of the little kids is saying that nothing ever happens around here, while in the background, in silhouette, kids from past ages and cultures are everywhere: Indian children playing war games, Pilgrim children doing chores, depression-era kids playing marbles, kids playing with hula hoops, cabbage patch dolls and computers. It's all in how you look at it.

If you walk down to the eastern end of 42nd Street, you can see the sparkling glass of the United Nations Plaza, where hundreds of nations have had millions of arguments in thousands of languages. Turn your head north a little more than 90 degrees and you can see where King Kong was shot off the Empire State building. I walked down Fifth, past the block where Teddy Roosevelt grew up and learned to be 'bully,' past the building where my uncle ran a freight elevator for 31 years, past Union Square, site of the draft riots during the Civil War, and past Washington Square Park where we used to dig for Indian skeletons. In my neighborhood, where the traffic lights give way to stop signs, and cobblestones poke through the blacktop, I weaved my way through a four block *Walk for Multiple Sclerosis*, and turned onto Spring Street. I live in SoHo, just south of Houston Street, just north of Wall Street, right next door to the Bowery, and about a hundred years past its prime. It's been a neighborhood of immigrants, of artists, of real estate developers, of survivors. SoHo, like a lot of New York, is a world that just keeps rebuilding itself from the inside out.

My building, scrubbed and painted just a few years ago, is on the corner of Spring and Varick. It's only six stories, a dwarf in this city, but it has character. There are two lofts per floor, and mine is on the south side of the top floor. I wanted that one because if you position yourself just about halfway along the south window and look west, you can see a small rectangle of the Hudson River. I always get a feeling of power when I'm looking down on water. Actually, I get that feeling when I'm looking down on anything.

There were no messages on my machine, thank you very much, so I went into the music room with my sax and started blowing. Now Charley Parker, there was a detective. He could find a clue and chase it through the most complex tune. He could sniff out a riff, arrest it and make it do time. He could, but I can't. I've been hyperventilating into this horn for seven years, and everything still sounds like "Pennies from Heaven." Musicians like him play music, and the rest of us play songs.

I love this room, though. The music room was my first renovation project after moving in, when it was still pretty much an empty warehouse in an almost empty building. Before the kitchen, before the parakeet cage, before the sleeping area, before the wall, I chose a corner of my 6000 square foot sanctuary to convert into a music room. I built it in an irregular shape, a rectangle with a corner missing, creating one long diagonal wall, not out of esthetic reasons, but just to see if I could do it. Soundproofing came next, at the firm request of some non-saxophone loving neighbors, and then track lighting, cabinets for my stereo equipment and thick carpeting. It took me three weeks, and I remember how great I felt when I finished it. It was the smallest room in the place, and I was still sleeping on the floor, but after living here for almost six months, I finally felt like I was home.

After dinner, I started looking through the notebook I had copied. Walter Rupert was not a faithful diarist. He started it on January 1st, 1974, and there was a brief entry every day for a few weeks, then once a week, and then only sporadically for the next few years. Nor was it the stuff of epic literature. He wrote about his work, his aches and pains and the frustration of growing old, about fear of the future. Most of the later entries seemed to start with bad weather or a bill he couldn't pay or something he saw, heard or read that infuriated him. He ranted about politics, about immigrants, about taxes, and about crime. It surprised me to learn he really was an unhappy man, despite the cheerful side of him I had always seen.

After an entry that read, 'Yes! Reagan will do it! We'll finally get this country moving and get some respect for its older citizens!,' I started scanning quickly, and then flipping through from the back, until I found a reference to THE BOOK.

"September 12. Out of the blue, a phone call and an argument with P. about THE BOOK. After all these years, HERITAGE becomes important.

"September 18. This system. The hippie kids used to call it a monster, and they were right. This system keeps me ragged and hungry, and I'm sick of it. God forgive me, I'm thinking of selling THE BOOK. I know it's dangerous, and I know it's wrong, but it's all I have.

"September 19. Called two book dealers. They won't tell me anything over the phone, but there's a bunch of dealers near 14th

Street I can visit. By Monday, I may be a rich man, but what a price to pay.

"September 22. I'm sorry I ever lived to this age. Poppa, I'm almost glad you died when you did. Thieves and liars! Seven stores I went to. Seven stores and seven liars. But I won't give up. I will not be cheated.

"Tuesday, September 23. Finally, some interest. They're still playing cute, but I know their game. The five hundred is only the beginning. It's just a matter of time now."

Another entry, undated, read, "I met the future today, and it's dark, dangerous and terrible to consider. I've taken precautions, though. I'm ready."

That was the last entry. Wednesday, the 24th, was the night he died. Maybe he wasn't as ready as he thought.

Four

The next morning, I returned the original of Mr. Rupert's diary to Paulie, along with a prune Danish and coffee, extra light no sugar, and told him about what I had read. The kitchen was as dark and dusty as the rest of the apartment, and my elbows kept sticking to the tablecloth. There was a big oak breakfront with all the dishes neatly stacked in it, except for the higher shelves. The appliances all looked to be about World War II vintage. There was a constant hum from the refrigerator, and a very faint odor of gas.

"I guess that shows I wasn't crazy about the book," Paulie said through a half smile. He sipped carefully at his coffee and nibbled around the edges of his Danish.

"It shows a few other things, too," I said. "It proves none of the experts thought it was valuable."

"Someone did have an interest, though. He got that offer of five hundred dollars. Here, on the twenty-third, just like I said."

"It also shows he had an argument with 'P' over the book just a few days before he died. That wasn't you, was it?"

He shook his head. "No, it wasn't me. In the last few weeks, Walter has had more violent fits of temper than in the previous ten years. He yelled at me a lot, but I never yelled back. That's a mercy."

"Can you think of anyone with the initial 'P' that might have called him out of the blue and talked about the book?"

He smoothed the long strands of white hair across his head. "'P?' No. There was a Mrs. Piccolo on six for a while, but she's been gone for a few years now."

"Do you know where I can get in touch with her? It isn't much, but it's a lead."

He tilted his head the slightest bit and almost smiled at me. "No, not gone away," he said quietly. "Gone."

"Oh," I said, feeling stupid. I wished I had a pipe to light or a gun to twirl or a dame to kiss. I was trying to be a detective and he wasn't helping at all. "Did he ever talk about heritage? That was in capital letters in his diary."

"Oho," he chuckled. "Heritage. Yes, all the time, like it was the Holy Grail, like it was precious as air. His heritage was the single most important thing in the world to Walter. Too important, I think. It cost him dearly, in the end. It cost him his wife and his daughter."

"I gathered from the journal that he wasn't really a very happy man."

He leaned back, folded his hands across his belly and looked up at the ceiling. That was his bard pose. I had seen it before, and I knew it meant a long story was coming, so I just sat back and listened.

He began slowly, his voice stronger and deeper, as if it originated from somewhere in his past. "There's a time in every man's life that's magical, Arthur, when every dream comes true, when there's no past or future, only the here and now. But it's a brief time, and most men only realize how brief their summer is when they look back on it from the December of old age. Some men are able to let it go but remember it clearly and cherish it. Unfortunately, some men can't let it go and the fading magic spoils and turns sour. Instead of reminding them to have pride in what they were, it tortures them with what they no longer are.

"Walter's magical time was his boyhood, growing up in Brooklyn Heights, working in his father's carpentry shop. It was another era, almost a different world then. People still had values, they had family around them, they had optimism. It was before drugs and race and greed began to strip off the veneer of civilization. Think of it for a moment, Arthur. Think of the glory of being eighteen and strong, working next to your father, shoulder to shoulder, and earning his respect. Imagine courting a woman and proving yourself by creating a family. It's pure glory, Arthur. It's pure intoxicating glory. It's almost God. Youth, Arthur. Youth is a deity that's only prayed to in old age."

He stopped and stared at some point between us with glazed, faraway eyes. I was almost too lost to notice, trying to remember what I had felt like at eighteen.

"Give me a minute and I'll show you the heart and soul of Walter Rupert." He pulled himself up carefully, walked down the hallway to Walter's room, and came back with one of the dusty photographs from his dresser. It showed a huge, brightly lit, open platform. Tables and tools were scattered all around, and in the background, far below the platform, was water; the ocean or a bay. In the faded black and white photograph, there were about a dozen men in shirtsleeves, baggy pants and work aprons. Several of them wore hats; most had their sleeves rolled up. Some were intent on their work, and some were looking at the camera. To the left, dwarfing everyone and everything else in the picture, was the huge metallic head and pointed crown of one of the most easily recognized symbols in the world.

Paulie pointed a bony finger at one of the men. "That one there is Walter's grandfather, and the young man just turning toward the camera is Walter's father. They worked together on the crew that assembled the Statue of Liberty, right here in New York Harbor, sometime in the 1880s. Imagine the pride that comes with that, Arthur. Imagine boasting that your father and your grandfather built the Statue of Liberty. That was part of Walter's heritage, too. He learned his trade from his father, and he captured some of the pride and glory of those years in the furniture shop with him. But Walter could never let the glory fade. That was his biggest problem. He could never let the past go. As he got older, he became more and more resistant to change. I guess he became arrogant. He pined for the past and raged against anything new and different. His stubborn resistance to the real world alienated his wife and daughter, and he ended up alone."

"Not quite alone," I said, after a moment. "He had a good friend in you."

He smiled at me. "Yes, that's true, he did. And now I'm alone."

We sat quietly for a few moments with that funeral feeling again, knowing the most sincere and heartfelt words are meaningless against the harsh reality of death.

What is it like to be his age? I wondered. What is it like to know you haven't got enough time to do the things you want to do? Most of us have a dream, a Camelot, something that makes us lean forward when the wind gets strong. Someone Paulie's age had either reached his dream long ago, or was plagued by the knowledge that he never would. There was always a sadness about him, a sorrow and complacency just beneath his smile. Whatever his dream was, I don't think it ever came true. He worked for thirty years in the token booth of a noisy, fetid subway station...not exactly the stuff dreams are made of.

"I need to know more," I said quietly. "About the book, about his family, about him."

He smiled at me slyly. Yes, it's possible to smile slyly even when you're missing teeth. "You're starting to believe me, aren't you?"

That poodle straddling my leg again. "I believe there is a book," I said, "and I believe Mr. Rupert considered it valuable. But questions keep piling up. Why didn't he know why it was valuable, and why didn't those book dealers think it was valuable? I can't believe they were all thieves and liars, or conspiring to cheat him. And why did he think it was wrong, and dangerous, to sell the book? Who else thought it was valuable enough to steal? And I guess the most important question is, 'Where is it'?"

Paulie took a deep breath, an accomplishment at his age. "Well, it's not in his room," he said. "I'm sure of that. After you left yesterday, I looked everywhere. Under things, behind things, on top of things. It just isn't in there. I spent three hours looking, and three hours of doing anything is a lot for me." He did look more than usually pale and tired.

I took the journal from him and flipped through it, shook it and tossed it on the table. "Can you describe the book to me?"

He closed his eyes and tilted his head up, like he was going into a trance. "It's reddish, almost maroon colored, but faded, I guess. You would be faded too if you were that old. Let me think—it's in pretty good condition except for a little stain."

"Where did the stain come from?"

He shrugged his shoulders. "I have no idea. Maybe water. It's just a dark maroon spot, darker than the rest of the cover."

"How big is it? The book, not the stain."

He started gesturing with his hands, and I reached for the journal to give him something to compare with. As I reached, I noticed a single word written on the inside back cover of the notebook, 'sirloined!'

Paulie had reached over to the counter and held up the Betty Crocker cookbook. "Just about this size, maybe a little smaller," he said.

I showed him the writing on the back of the journal. "Is that Mr. Rupert's handwriting?"

He adjusted his glasses and looked at it carefully. "Why, yes, I think it is. What an odd word to write. I wonder what it means?"

"Maybe he planned to celebrate with a good steak."

"Steak, what do you mean steak?" He looked between me and the word on the cover again. "Oh, 'sirloined.' I thought it said 'purloined.'"

"Purloined?" I said. "That's a letter 'P.' Purloined means stolen. Could the book have been stolen before he was killed? When was the last time you saw it?"

"I haven't seen it for almost a year. He usually got nostalgic around Christmas and brought it out of its hiding place. But I did see him leaving the other morning with a brown package, I guess about the size of a book, and he came back with it the same afternoon. I remember because it wasn't the blue bag."

"The blue bag? What blue bag?"

"When he trotted the book out on holidays, it was always in this blue velvet bag, but not this time. But it was the right size, and I can only assume it was *Pilgrim's Progress*."

"That was which morning, Tuesday or Wednesday?"

He got a pained expression on his face. "Oh, let me think a moment. My memory has gotten so bad." He thumped his forehead lightly with the heel of his hand. "It was three mornings ago, so that would have been Tuesday. Yes. No. It was Wednesday, because when he came home, he interrupted *The Today Show* the day Jane Pauley had the whole cast of *Days of Our Lives*, and he shouted at me to turn it off. Yes, Wednesday, I'm sure."

"So, if he still had it on Wednesday, the day he was killed, what was purloined? And why use a word like 'purloined'? Wasn't there a story...yeah, *The Purloined Letter*. Mark Twain, maybe? Charles Dickens?"

"No," Paulie said. "It was an Edgar Allen Poe story. I'm sure of it."

"Right. *The Purloined Letter*. Edgar Allan Poe. Can I get one of the books from Mr. Rupert's room?"

"No, no. Let me get it," Paulie said. "It's such a mess in there now." He shuffled down the hallway again and came back with the Poe collection that contained the story, *The Purloined Letter*.

"I used to tell this story to school children," he said. "In a scaled down version, of course."

"I'm not sure if this is meaningful or not," I said, "but I don't know where else to look right now. I'm going to go home and read this. Maybe Mr. Rupert was trying to tell us something."

"Well, that was Walter all over. Always telling someone something." As he walked me to the door, Paulie said, "I will see you Monday morning, won't I?"

"Uh, Monday morning?" I asked.

"The funeral. He's being laid out at Cooke's on 98th Street, and the service will be at St. Margaret's, ten-thirty sharp. You will be there, won't you?"

"Well, I don't know. I was planning to start...um, of course. Sure, I'll be there." I had other plans, but I figured I could put off canvassing the bookstores until after the funeral. It's not like I was looking forward to it.

I had worn my sneakers and old sweats, so I walked home again. This time the walk was for exercise. I gave up jogging in favor of power walking about two years ago, and my knees and feet take less of a pounding and are much less sore after a workout. You just have to get into a rhythm when you power walk. Heel down, rock to the toe. Elbows close to the body, keep the hips straight and rotate the trunk. I had a good sweat by 42nd Street, and slowed to a stroll by Houston Street.

I took the back elevator up, the clunky, old freight elevator, using my key to open the big horizontal doors, and was greeted by the chattering dialogue of Lancelot and Guinevere.

My dad owned this place before his big crash. He bought it at a very good price just before SoHo became trendy, and, like Allan predicted, it has appreciated steeply ever since. I don't think either of them ever set foot in it. In fact, I don't know if either of them ever set foot in SoHo. Allan preferred the glass and flash of midtown, and Dad liked the give and take of condescension and sycophancy you find in City Hall. He signed it over to me as a gift for my 30th birthday and despite its origin story, it is legally mine. I am 'The Loft Lizard.' I thought for a little while about selling it, but it is home now. Home.

After a shower and lunch, I sat down with the book of Poe's short stories. *The Purloined Letter*, subtitled *Nil sapientiae odiosius acrimine nimio*, and who can argue with that? My high school Latin was able to translate it as something like 'Nobody likes a smart ass,' but it may require a little more nuance. *The Purloined Letter* was basically a detective story. In fact, it is considered to be one of the world's first detective stories. In it, an important and sensitive letter has been stolen and is being used for blackmail in 19th century Paris. The thief is known, and it is also known that the letter is kept somewhere in his apartment, but cannot be found. After months of extensive and futile search, the Prefect of Parisian Police, what a great job title, asks our detective, C. August Dupin, for his help. Using only his reasoning powers, Dupin finds the letter in the apartment, on a desk among other cards and letters. The moral of the story is that the letter was hidden, as simply as possible, in plain sight. Hmm.

Was Mr. Rupert telling us he hid the book somewhere so obvious it would take a real detective to find it, or was he really just thinking about a good piece of steak?

~ * ~

I thought it best to let my subconscious work on that question for a while, so I changed into an old shirt and coveralls and did some work on my latest project, the wall. I've been stripping the plaster from this sixty-by-ten-foot wall in fits and starts for a couple of months, afraid to really get into it because of the mess it makes. Fine plaster dust hangs in the air for days, and eventually settles onto everything in the whole loft. It doesn't seem to make much difference how careful I am covering things up; the white powder penetrates and settles everywhere. Despite the inconvenience, I had made up my mind... today was the day.

I taped thick plastic drop cloths to the ceiling and anchored them to the floor with some wood left over from the birdcage. That shut me off in a five-foot wide walkway almost the whole sixty-foot length of the wall. I put on my gloves, goggles and mask, connected the compressor to the sand blaster, pointed to a dingy white section and let her rip. Within seconds, the sand and plaster dust was so thick I could just barely see the spray from the nozzle. I squinted and held the spray as steady as I could, and in about twenty minutes had stripped the plaster off a section of wall about four feet by six feet. There's a brick wall behind all of that plaster. Not the smooth, massed produced brick we're used to today; the old kind of rough, handmade, red brick, mortared in by a master bricklayer when someone's dream was for this place to be a bustling sweatshop. I think it was hats, or maybe gloves they made here. Maybe both.

I felt a strong need to get it done before I move out, if I move out, and I figured I could just clean everything as I packed. I assumed if I went west with Jonesy, I would have to sell the place. It wasn't rentable in its half-finished condition. After twelve years and a lot of sweat—I mean a *lot* of sweat—I would be walking away from it. Damn! Three or four more years and I might have been finished.

I suppose in a way it is fitting. The man who gave it to me was unfinished. He was always running after something else, something new. Our relationship remains unfinished, because while he was running, I chose not to keep up with him. Now this loft may never be finished. An intact circle of unfinished business.

So, I was determined to cross this wall off my to-do list. I put the mask and goggles on, took a deep breath, and blasted away. The phone rang and I didn't even hear the pitch for whatever she was selling. When I got hungry, I ordered in Thai food. When it got dark, I set up some lamps. My arms and hands cramped, so I took short breaks and stretched. By midnight, I was standing in about an eighth of an inch of sand and plaster, and couldn't see more than five feet, but the wall was done. I now had 600 square feet of solid brick in my living room.

There, Dad. I finished something. Your turn.

~ * ~

The first thing Paulie did when he saw me at the funeral the next day was to brush what he thought was dandruff from the shoulder of my blue jacket. St. Margaret's is a gothic, old-fashioned church, all spikes and spires on the outside, and all polished wood and vaulted ceilings on the inside. The dark wood casket, small and silent, stationed just in front of the altar, was at the center of the church. I've always thought of a casket as an elevator you lie down in. You go either up or down, but you're not the one who presses the button. I guess that's the legacy of a Catholic school education. After all these years, Sister Saint Philomena and the Baltimore Catechism still have a grip on me.

"I'm glad you're here a few minutes early," Paulie said, brushing off my shoulder. "There's someone I'd like you to meet."

He steered me over to a stout woman with frosted blonde-gray hair and a double chin. "This is Marguerite, ah, Emerson, I think. Yes, Emerson now, but always my little Marguerite. Arthur is the detective friend I was telling you about. He'll help us find out what really happened."

Her handshake was cool, and her smile brief and shallow. One of those, 'I suppose it's nice to meet you, but it's obvious you're a member of an inferior species' kind of smiles. She was well dressed...very well dressed, I would say. I don't have a clue about women's clothes, but there is something unmistakable about expensive things.

"Marguerite is Walter's daughter," Paulie said, beaming at her. "I haven't seen her in probably thirty years, and doesn't she look just great." Another surprise. Paulie could actually gush.

I was granted another puddle deep smile. "It's good of you to come, Mr. McCullough," she said. "As you probably know, my father and I had been estranged for quite some time.

"Yes," I said. "But since Paulie has asked me to investigate your father's death, I wonder if we could have coffee sometime, somewhere and discuss a few things. Even a phone conversation would help."

"The book," she said with a smile. A real smile this time—deep, wide and unfathomable. "Yes, of course. Perhaps it would be better if you called me at home. Tomorrow or the next day. Uncle Paul, Paulie, has my number."

She looked at me a moment longer, so I felt I had to say it. "I'm sorry about your father."

"Yes," she said. "Thank you. I am too, now." She gave Paulie a kiss on the cheek and slowly made her way into one of the pews. There she grasped the hand of the woman next to her, and slowly lowered her face into the other hand.

There were only a few of us in attendance: Mr. Rupert's daughter and her companion, Paulie and I, and perhaps another half-dozen senior citizens.

Paulie whispered introductions, always referring to me as 'the detective,' and they were all quite pleased to meet me. I didn't sense real grief in any of them, or awe at their surroundings. This was their space. A funeral in an empty church was as natural to them as a video game to a fifteen-year-old.

I disengaged myself, with difficulty, from Paulie when the service began. I stayed in the last pew, standing when the others stood, kneeling when they knelt. Mrs. Emerson occasionally glanced around and scanned the back of the church, nervously. *Another backslider waiting for lightning to strike,* I thought.

The priest was elderly as well. He moved cautiously and his hands trembled when he blessed us. The sermon was mercifully brief and probably not too great a variation from the usual funeral message.

Good man, full life, greater reward, someday it will be our turn. I was a little concerned that Paulie would give a eulogy, and turn it into a three-act drama, but that was not on the playbill.

Pallbearers from the funeral home, apparently not trusting the physical abilities of the dearly beloved the departed left behind, loaded Mr. Rupert's mortal remains into the limo for the long ride to the cemetery in Brooklyn.

Paulie rode in the limo with Mrs. Emerson and her friend, and I made excuses as best I could. I had already decided my day would be better spent talking with book dealers. Besides, I can't do tears. I really can't.

I hopped an express train to 14th Street, checking first to be sure I had those business cards from Mr. Rupert's hidey-hole.

Fourteenth Street on the East side has seen it all, and much of it is still there to see. It's kind of a Jewish, Black-Hispanic, residential-commercial, upper-middle-lower, tourist-blue collar kind of neighborhood, which is always bustling except when it's deserted. For some reason, probably a good reason, a lot of antiquarian booksellers had set up shop in that area over the years. In the West Village, streets crisscross and intersect at acute angles. By guesswork and dead reckoning, and making a series of random left turns, I found my way to the Grove St. Bookstore, a narrow building squeezed between a construction site and a discount electronics store. A smudged sign in the front window said:

Monday-Friday 9AM to 8PM
Saturday, 10AM to 6PM

It looked musty and neglected, and although it was Monday, it was dark, locked and closed.

The next bookstore on my list, The Sage, was just around the corner. It was, in contrast to the Grove Street, 'a clean, well-lighted place' inhabited by two clerks, one unpacking a box, and another checking receipts at the cash register. An older man was sitting at a table looking carefully at a book.

"I wonder if you can help me," I said to the guy at the register. "I was given your card by an acquaintance who was in here sometime last week. He was trying to sell a copy of *Pilgrim's Progress*." The clerk looked at me and then nodded toward the man at the table, apparently the man in charge.

"I do remember that gentleman." The older man smiled. He was stocky and round faced, with a couple of days' worth of white stubble. "Got mad as hell when I told him his book was almost worthless. Called me all sorts of names, too."

"Can you tell me anything about the book?" I asked.

"What was it he called me?" he said to the clerk behind the counter.

"I remember he said 'buzzard'," the clerk answered.

"He called me a capitalist marionette."

"Can you tell me anything about the book?" I asked again.

"A capitalist marionette," he laughed. "Who says things like that anymore?"

"Is there anything you can tell me about the book?" I asked a little louder than I meant to.

"I guess I can," he said, "but I don't see any reason why I should. Who the hell are you and why do you want to know?"

I dug through my wallet and showed him my license. He glanced at it, spectacularly unimpressed.

"The man's name was Walter Rupert, and he was killed the other day," I said. "A close friend of his feels the book has something to do with the murder."

"My name is Bernard Prowse," he said. He looked at me for a long moment with absolutely no expression. He was probably wondering, like I was, if a book could be the cause of someone's death.

"I have been in this business for almost twenty years, and I don't make mistakes. The book," he said firmly, "was not worth more than ten dollars. Granted, in this city ten bucks probably could be a motive for murder, especially if you're too old to defend yourself."

"Mr. Prowse," I asked, "was there anything at all special about it? Anything that remotely could have made it valuable?"

He shook his head impatiently. "No, no. That book has been published in a thousand editions, most of them better quality than the one I saw. There were probably no more than a few thousand units in that Corbin edition."

"Corbin edition?"

"Yes. Corbin and Son. A Brooklyn-based publisher in the late 19th century. The *Pilgrim's Progress* your friend brought in here was a Corbin and Son."

"Can you tell me anything else about it? Were there any distinguishing features?"

He rubbed his forehead and breathed deeply. I got a faint odor of alcohol.

"I see a lot of books every day, and as I already told you, this one was unremarkable. I don't know what else I can tell you. I see no reason for that book to figure in a murder." He snorted and went back to the book he had been studying.

"Another dealer offered him five hundred for it. At least that's what I was told."

"What kind of dealer? Around here?"

"Yes. Grove Street Bookstore."

"I don't know that operation, but no one with even a rudimentary knowledge of books would value that one at five hundred bucks. Somebody's lying to you, my friend."

"Well, thanks anyway," I said. I know I was supposed to give him my business card and say, 'If you think of anything else, give me a call,' but it seemed like a waste of time.

"I'm sorry about your friend," he called as I got near the door. "I liked him. I like feisty old men and there aren't enough of us left, but that book was worthless."

I got a similar message at three other shops I tried, and two others didn't remember Walter until I prompted them with a description. Those two remembered some salty language, but didn't recall the book at all. I checked once more, but the Grove Street Bookstore was still crumbling, still dark, and still locked.

My feet were pinched and crampy from my funeral shoes, so I took the subway home. The trip had not been a total loss. I had established there really was a *Pilgrim's Progress* and that Walter Rupert had tried to sell it at some of the bookstores last week. On the other hand, it was increasingly certain the experts had seen the book as essentially worthless. Why had Walter been so sure they were wrong?

The idiot light was flashing on my answering machine, but I waited until I had showered and put my funeral suit back into deep storage before tapping the playback button. After the first two bars of "Blackbird" and my 'Guess I'm out now, but at least you can leave a message,' I heard the frantic and hyperventilating voice of Paulie.

"Arthur, are you there? He came back! You have to call me. Call me, Arthur, please?"

I found the number and called back as quickly as I could, but there was no answer. I finished changing and took a cab uptown to his apartment. There were an ambulance and a police car in front of his building, and a small crowd of neighbors craning their necks to see who had died. I lied to one of the cops that I was related to Paulie. I bolted up the five flights just as he was being carried out on a stretcher, strapped down under a neatly folded blanket, oxygen mask over his face, his eyes wide and frightened.

I didn't even try to talk to him. I just whispered, "I'm here, Paulie. I get it now, and I'll stay as long as I need to." I thought he smiled, or at least wrinkled his face a little, but under the oxygen mask it was hard to tell.

Jesus, I thought. *Maybe this is for real.*

Five

The door to his apartment was open halfway, and I heard soft sobbing inside. I stepped carefully from the gloomy, threatening hallway into the light-streaked cavern that had been Paulie's home. Inside, a uniformed cop with red hair and a wispy mustache wandered around looking things over. He was chuckling softly and shaking his head slowly. An elderly woman, vaguely familiar to me, was wringing something in her hands and crying, looking back and forth from the cop to the floor in front of her. For some reason, my appearance seemed to make her feel better.

"He just collapsed," she grabbed my arm as I came through the door. "There was nothing I could do." Her eyes pleaded with me to understand it wasn't her fault. I was only able to nod.

"What can I do for you?" the cop asked. I showed him my license, this time without feeling self-conscious or silly.

"I'm a friend of Mr. Dwyer," I said, and then added, "He's a client. What happened to him?"

"The resident, a Mr. Paul Dwyer, apparently had a visitor while he was out. The window had been jimmied, and his bedroom had been, uh, burglarized. I guess you could call it 'burglarized.' When the

53

resident returned and saw what happened, he became over-excited and collapsed."

"Heart attack?" I asked.

He shook his head. "The EMTs didn't think so. Just stress, anxiety, hyperventilation. They said he'll probably be okay after he calms down and gets some rest. They took him to Metropolitan Hospital for observation, mostly as a precaution, I think."

"I came home from the cemetery early. I was taking a nap when he came to my apartment to get me," the old woman said, still clinging to my arm. She had deep, perfectly spaced, perfectly symmetrical lines running down from her scalp, across her cheeks to her lips, like a textbook picture of the magnetic lines of the earth. "He was breathing so hard and so noisy he couldn't talk," she said. "As soon as he showed me the room, he collapsed and I called the police."

I held her hand on my arm, walked down the hall like a bride and groom from Edgar Allen Poe, and pushed opened the door to Mr. Rupert's room.

I was so surprised I almost laughed out loud. Nothing had been broken, nothing had been damaged. Everything had simply been taken apart. The rug had been rolled up and dragged off to one side, and all the furniture—chairs, bed, table, lamps, dresser—had been broken down into pieces and placed in piles at the far end of the room. All the books were in neat stacks in the middle of the room and the book jackets were piled a few feet away. The contents of the closet and dressers had been placed on the mattress, still folded and in neat piles. Nothing appeared to be damaged, or even tossed around carelessly. This had not been done violently, but carefully.

The cop came up behind us. "It looks like he broke through the window frame with a crowbar and then just started taking things apart." He pointed to a small pile of nuts, bolts and screws. "Used a saw too, and even put the sawdust into the garbage pail. I've never seen anything like it."

"What's the procedure for you?" I asked.

"Just the standard operational bull, um, procedure." He shrugged. "Write it up as a burglary, get a list of missing items when the resident gets back home. But I've been looking around the rest of the apartment, and none of the usual stuff seems to be missing. You know, like jewelry, cash, electronics. In fact, I don't think the rest of the apartment was even touched. To do all of this…carpentry, he probably didn't have time to rob the rest of the place. Doesn't make a lot of sense to me."

"It only makes sense," I said mostly to myself, "if someone knew exactly what he was looking for and was pretty sure it was in this room."

The woman next to me began to weep again. "This neighborhood. I'm getting so scared," she said softly.

"I'll tell you something, lady," he said. "One of the first things I learned as a cop…insure everything. You just never can tell."

"Can you make sure Detective Chasko gets a copy of your report," I said to the cop. "There was a murder here a few days ago that he insists was a suicide. This may change his mind."

The cop nodded. "I know a Chasko. Detective in the twentieth, right? Okay. I'll tell him, if he'll grant me an audience."

"Is there any problem with me staying here tonight?" I asked. "I'd like to poke through this stuff and try to figure some things out."

"I've met him before," the old lady told the cop. "I'll vouch that he's a friend of Mr. Dwyer's."

"That's good enough for me, if you let me take another look at that PI license. And it might make Mrs. Federico feel better," he said, nodding at the woman. Mrs. Federico. The name, like her face, rang a distant bell. "But I should warn you," he said. "Keep on your toes. Sometimes these sumbitches come back."

I got Mrs. Federico calmed down and walked her back to her apartment. I remembered now I had met her at the funeral and she told me her husband used to be a detective when they lived in Los Angeles. She had a very faint scent of perfume, kind of vanilla-ish, and her clenched hands had the pale puffiness of dinner rolls. "He's such a good man, Mr. Dwyer," she sniffed into her tissue. "I hope he'll be all right."

"Do you know him well?" I asked, suddenly the detective again. "Did you know Mr. Rupert well?"

"Yes. I've lived here for seven years now, and I know them both quite well. They used to have me over to dinner occasionally; sometimes I would have them over to my place. It gets so lonely, living by yourself."

"They were such close friends," I said. "It must be hard for Paulie to be without Mr. Rupert."

"Yes, hard," she smiled at me. "But easy, too. They didn't always get along so well together, you know. There was a lot of competition and tension. We sometimes had dinners with hardly a word between them, they were both so angry at each other."

"What were they competing for?"

"Who knows what? They're men. Even though they're old, they still act like men. One liked the Yankees, the other liked the Jets. Walter liked coffee, Paul only drinks tea. They would fight about almost anything."

"Did they get loud?"

"Oh, Walter would. He would yell the most outrageous things at Paul. Not curses. He was never profane. Just name-calling. Things like 'potato head,' 'bog Irish,' 'immigrant.' Things that seem kind of silly to most people, but you could see they hurt Paul."

"And Paulie wouldn't yell back?"

"No, he would just sit and pout. The madder he got, the quieter he got. No, I don't think I ever heard him raise his voice. Well, except for one time. But I'm not sure I should tell you about that."

"One time?" I asked.

"This one night...oh, maybe a month ago. I can't remember ever seeing a man get that mad. I thought Paul would have a heart attack. His face was so red and he was shaking and yelling at Walter. I...I think he may have threatened to push Walter out the window."

Whoa.

"What Did Mr. Rupert do to get him so angry?"

She smiled coyly. "Walter asked me to marry him. I turned him down, of course. It never could have worked out." She leaned over and whispered to me, "I was a little afraid of him. He killed his first wife, you know."

I walked slowly back to Paulie's apartment, trying to build a mental picture of him throwing someone out a window. I picked through all the hardware and lumber in Walter's build-it-yourself bedroom, trying to see what the burglar might have seen, trying to see what Walter might have seen, trying to see anything from someone else's point of view. That's the secret of a happy life, someone once told me...look at things from the other person's point of view. I thumped on the walls, stamped on the floor, felt around the door jambs, and looked carefully around the empty closet. Nothing. Not a clue, not an inkling.

Paulie's bedroom was a little smaller, more sparsely furnished and a little brighter. His bed was made, his medicine was lined up neatly on his dresser, and he had a list of things to do taped on his mirror. 'Water plants,' 'Mr. D. about heat,' and 'change for laundry,' had the highest priority. Next to the list there was a picture I had seen before. It showed Paulie, distracted and embarrassed, holding hands with Mrs. Federico.

I wrestled with the idea for a few moments, and then I called Jonesy to leave a message on her machine that I would be here. She was almost never home in the afternoon, it being prime beauty parlor and/or shopping time, and I was caught off guard when she answered in person.

"Oh, hi," I said. "How would you like an adventure?"

"Anytime, anywhere," she answered. "By the way, who is this?"

"Ha, ha. I'm serious. An adventure."

"Dining, cinematic or sexual?" she asked.

"The real thing. I want you to spend the night with me in an apartment where a murder and a burglary have taken place."

She hesitated a moment. "Not your old man friend, Paul?"

"Paulie. No, he's okay, but I'm at his apartment. He collapsed this afternoon and was taken to the hospital. It's just for observation they tell me, so I thought I'd spend the night here. Sort of be a detective. Can you make it? There's a lot I want to tell you."

"Give me the address," she said excitedly. "I want to bring some cameras."

"Bring dinner, too," I said. "Chinese or Italian. Adventure makes me hungry."

She didn't even take the time to give me one of those back pat/hugs when I let her in. She handed me the brown bags with dinner and started stalking the apartment, mumbling something about light. She pulled a camera out of its bag, snapped off a long lens and snapped on a short one.

"This place is a regular catacomb," she said, crouched in a corner and panning the room with the camera. "The way the sunbeams play tricks with the dust in here. And that faded paint. I wonder what color that used to be. Love those spidery cracks, too. Very Edgar Allen Poe."

"Here's where the action is," I said, opening the door to Mr. Rupert's bedroom.

"This is like a storeroom, right?"

"No, until recently, this was Mr. Rupert's bedroom. Those piles over there are the bed and dresser."

"My God. What happened here? What in the altogether hell? What twilight zone did you get yourself into?"

"So far, it's just burglary and murder, but there's always a chance something really interesting will happen. Remember last week I was telling you about Mr. Rupert's copy of *Pilgrim's Progress* and how Paulie thinks he may have been killed by someone who wanted it?"

"I remember you saying something about it," she said. "But I probably wasn't listening."

I laughed, sort of. Maybe that was the secret of our relationship. I could do no wrong because she wasn't paying much attention to me. But then I couldn't do anything especially right either, because she wasn't paying much attention to me. Balance is the core of a happy relationship.

I explained it all again, the suicide/murder, the cop with the *How to Win Friends and Influence People* attitude, and the book. That damned book. First it existed only in the memory of two old men, then it took on a life of its own when Walter Rupert landed on the pavement. It faded into myth when six experts in the field told me it had no value, but now it was real again. As real as the piles of wood in his room. I told her about the funeral, Mrs. Emerson, the booksellers, Paulie's undignified exit, and Mrs. Federico's neutron bomb.

"So, then, we're here now because...?" she asked when I finished. She was in the kitchen now, wrinkling her nose at the contents of Paulie's refrigerator. I wondered briefly what pears would look like through a pear-shaped lens.

"Because I don't know what else to do," I said honestly. "Because I need to get some kind of handle on what the hell is going on here. Because I need someone to talk this all through with, and because I haven't seen much of you in the past few days. And I may not be seeing you next week."

"You're pretty sure he won't come back."

"Sure, I'm sure," I said. "He had enough time here today to qualify as a tenant. What would he come back for?"

"I don't think I understand what he came for in the first place." She opened the cabinet under the sink. "Spic and Span. They still make that?"

"I think the guy who came here knows something or knows someone who knows something. Paulie thought he heard him ask Mr. Rupert something like 'Where is it?' And he referred to Paulie by name. Whoever came the second time knew Paulie was out and so he had plenty of time. And from the looks of that window, he didn't worry about sneaking in."

"I've read sometimes professional thieves check obituaries to find out when people will be out at a funeral." As she said that, I got a sudden flash of Mrs. Emerson looking around nervously in church.

"That's a good point. The funeral would be a perfect time to come. And when I went to that bookstore store this afternoon, it was closed. But your standard issue burglar doesn't generally dismantle rooms to find valuables," I said. "They look for cash, jewelry, electronics, stuff they can just grab and run. There's no reason to take furniture apart unless he was looking for something he knew was hidden in this room. And he was looking for a book, too, or else why separate books and book covers? I hate to admit it, because it's gonna complicate my life, but Paulie was right. Somebody out there wants that book, bad. Or, you could say somebody bad out there wants that book. Ha ha."

I spent some time looking around in the living room, turning over chairs and shaking lamps while she focused, snapped, advanced, and reloaded. "Aperture," she mumbled. "Depth of field. Natural light source."

After a while, we found plates and glasses and started dividing the Chinese food. "There is another explanation," she said over dim sum and red wine. "It might not be someone out there, it might be someone in here. It could be Paulie."

"What could be Paulie?"

"All of it. The whole pu pu platter, so to speak. He could have killed his roommate, covered it up with the story of a burglar, and made up the whole thing about the book."

"And did all that work in the next room?"

"Sure. I know it's a lot for someone his age, but he's had a couple of days, right? And he could have had an accomplice. Mrs. Fieldmouse maybe? Nah, not her."

"I guess it's possible," I said. "But why? What's the point?"

"Why do people kill other people? Isn't most of it some kind of domestic violence? Lovers' quarrels and stuff like that have nothing to do with age."

"I don't picture Walter and Paulie as gay."

"Or maybe it was over Mrs. Fenderbender down the hall you told me about. Or maybe they had just been together too long and were getting on each other's nerves. Look at this place. This atmosphere could make Mother Teresa push someone out a window."

"But then why play all these games? Why even bother to call me? The police had filed Mr. Rupert's death as a suicide. There was no need for Paulie to do all this work."

"Maybe he's guilt ridden and subconsciously wants to get caught. Maybe he's a schizo. Oh, wait, that's it. The book. Maybe he's been after the book all along, and he needs you to help him find it."

"Or, maybe he had nothing to do with it," I said. "Maybe the book is real and valuable, and everything happened just the way he said."

"Maybe. But then who's doing all this?" she asked. "And why do all of it if the book is worthless?"

"I don't know," I admitted. "I just can't get it to make sense. But I'm working on a theory."

"I just had a crazy idea," she said. "Definitely Hitchcock. You told me Paulie used to be a professional storyteller, right? Maybe he's doing it just for an adventure. He knows he's coming to the end of the trail and he wants to go out in a blaze of glory. If he's a frustrated old man who used to tell stories, maybe he's creating a story of his own to put a little excitement in his life."

"You don't know Paulie."

"Oh, and you do? You see the guy once a year to do his taxes, and talk on the phone maybe two other times a year. How well do you think you know him?"

I felt a draft, and got up to close the window in Walter's bedroom. The window frame had been pretty well mangled, but I managed to jam it into place well enough to hold together. The room immediately felt muggy and ancient.

After supper, we cleaned up and Jonesy started looking around through her camera lens again. "This place is like a photographer's classroom," she said. "The light in here is totally different than it was an hour ago, and it seems to change from room to room. These fabulous old buildings…"

"Are you going to do these up in a pear-shaped montage?" I asked, careful not to look at her. I can't imagine why I said that, I just remember I did.

"I know you think my photographs are silly," she said flatly, "but it's what I do."

She was busy arranging the door between the kitchen and the dining room. Move the door, three steps back, look carefully through the lens. Move the door two inches to the right, three steps back again, look up at the ceiling. Move the door again.

"I don't think the things you do are silly," I said. "I just don't understand some of them."

"You don't understand a lot of things. And I know you're not talking about my photography anymore, now you're talking about my going to Montana." There was a small catch in her voice, which I can't remember ever hearing before.

She glanced over at me, and I saw something peculiar in her face that matched her voice. Uncertainty. It wasn't so much that she was a strong woman, but I never knew her to pay the slightest attention to her weaknesses. I've seen her argue with cab drivers, fight for a seat on the subway, scalp tickets for a show, and send back a meal because it "just didn't taste right." I never did those things, any of them. She always had some kind of deep source of confidence that what she did would always be right, would always work out for her. But now, for the first time since I had known her, she was uncertain.

"What's bothering you?" I asked.

"Nothing. Life is just a bowl of damn cherries," she said with her back to me.

"Yeah, usually, but then sometimes it's a cabaret. Come on, it's me."

"Well," she said a little too loud. "I'm standing with my detective boyfriend, soon to be detective ex-boyfriend, in a horrid little apartment where a murder has just been committed, and I'm going to Montana in a few days to start a new life. And even my mother, the craziest person I know, thinks I'm crazy. What could possibly be bothering me?"

I skipped right over the 'mother' part of that message. "I know you don't really want to go way the hell out there," I said.

"Of course I don't want to go. But I don't want to not go. It's just that I know it's time for me to go. It's time for something." That book had it almost right. Men may be from Mars, but women are from a different galaxy altogether.

"What? What do you mean, 'time for you to go'?"

She sighed heavily and sat down. "I'm just not like you, Bird. I don't adapt to things the way you do. You're like a pigeon or something. You can live anywhere. I've been in Manhattan for sixteen years now, in ten different apartments, and never felt at home. My mother and I lived in four different cities before that, and I never felt at home in any of them, either. You didn't know I was from Harrisburg originally, did you?"

"Jonesy Shaw, the pride of Harrisburg, Pennsylvania." I laughed.

A dirty look. "Don't do that, *Arthur*. I'm trying to be honest with you, and it's hard. This is my life, bouncing from one place to another."

"Come on, Jonesy, you have a nice life here. I really don't get why you want to bounce."

She just shook her head. "Do you know the Eagles song, "Already Gone"? I haven't heard it in ten years, and I didn't like it back then. But I heard it on the radio the other day and, you know what? I knew every word. Every lick, every 'oh baby,' every 'whoo hoo hoo.'"

"Well, kudos for your long-term memory," I said, "but it doesn't mean anything. It's a song lyric some stoner wrote right after he got fired."

Another dirty look. "It's a sign. I know you think that's stupid, but that's all I can think of. Something from the cosmos, or something from the bottom of my brain, or a twinge in my trick knee. I don't know. I just think it's a sign that, somehow, I'm already gone."

"So, if I follow your logic, you're moving to Montana because you know the words to an old song?"

"God, sometimes you can be such a pissant."

As she glared at me, I heard a muffled, scraping noise coming from Mr. Rupert's bedroom. "Jesus," I whispered. "Get over here behind the couch."

We both fell to the floor and peeked around the arm of the couch. "What is it?" she asked me. "What do you think it is? The guy?"

It was getting dark in the living room now, and darker in Mr. Rupert's bedroom. I could see a light beam moving slowly around the room through the half-open door. "Go over to Mrs. Federico's," I whispered. "Across the hall and two doors down. Call the police. Tell them anything, but get them here quick." I pushed her toward the door, and edged around the couch, taking my shoes off. I waited a few minutes to give her enough time to get down the hall and make the call. 'Please, please, Jonesy, don't come back here. Stay with Mrs. whatever. Please.'

I wondered how long it would take for the cops to arrive. Bad neighborhood, five flights. Fifteen minutes? Thirty? More?

I tiptoed near the half-open door and listened for a minute. There was a soft thud and a creaking sound. I got down on all fours and peered in. A figure dressed all in black was kneeling on the floor in the far corner of the room with his back to me, intent on something in front of him. I pushed the door open a little more, and then a little more, until it was just wide enough for me to get through. I watched for a minute or two as he worked at something near the floor. In the dim light, there seemed to be a clear path between me and the dark figure, and without taking the time to make a decision, I ran at him as fast as I could. He was turning toward me just as my foot caught on something. I landed hard and bounced forward just far enough to grab him around the knees and pull him down. There was a flash of light, and something hard hit my head. He kicked at me and pulled away, jumping toward the window. I rolled over on my back and made a weak grab at him. Another flash blinded me for a second, and when my eyes cleared, the window was wide open and he was gone. I stumbled over to the window and looked out. There was a black clad figure moving quickly down the fire escape steps, and then swinging over to the dumpster. He hopped quickly off the dumpster, and was gone, a shadow at home in the shadows.

"Why the hell did I do that?" I groaned to myself. I hurt everywhere. When you're in your forties, you just can't go bouncing around on hardwood floors without paying a price. Jonesy was suddenly there, helping me sit up, but saying nothing. "Why did you come back here?" I yelled at her. "Didn't you call the cops?"

She shook her head, her eyes wide with fright, and then ran out of the room. I heard retching and coughing from the bathroom, and a few minutes later she walked quietly back in. "There was no one home over there," she said quietly. "I banged and shouted, but no one answered. I ran back to use this phone and I saw you jump up and run in here. I was just in time to see him whack you on the head with something and climb through the window. Is your head all right?"

"No. Yes. I don't know." I carefully fingered a sizable lump just behind my right ear. "How's your stomach?"

She smiled sheepishly, and then started to cry.

"My stupid fault," I said, wrapping my arms around her. "What the hell was I thinking? I thought he might come back. That cop even told me he might come back. Just stupid, stupid." We carried each other back into the living room and collapsed onto the couch. I squeezed and rubbed and made shushing noises until she was quiet and breathing softly, and then tiptoed back into the bedroom. I found the flashlight, still lit where it had fallen. An eight-foot section of floor molding lay in the middle of the room, probably with a dent in it the size and shape of my big toe, and another piece had been partially separated from the wall. "More carpentry. Now he's taking the molding off. Pretty soon this sneaky s.o.b. will have us down to the studs," I said to the ghosts of the three people who had recently experienced violence in this room. "What the hell was I thinking?"

Using the flashlight, I found a piece of heavy oak about the length of a baseball bat. I squatted in the corner, using the wall to prop up my head and my knees to keep the flashlight shining on the window. I stared at the window until the sun came up, and then fell asleep.

When I woke up, my foot ached almost as much as my head, and my head ached more than I thought possible. My first thought was the same as my last thought before falling asleep and I shouted it to an empty room. "What the hell was I thinking? What the hell is wrong with me? I can't find the goddamn book...I can't keep someone I love from leaving me? What the hell is wrong with me?"

I don't often practice self-pity, but I guess I don't have to. Sometimes it seems to come naturally.

I stretched slowly, scratched and limped out to the living room. Jonesy was just beginning to stir on the couch. I kissed her gently, and was reminded of the intimacy of bad breath. We sat and stared for a minute or two and I said, "A walk might do us both good. Why don't we go get some breakfast?"

The day was bright but chilly, and neither of us spoke. The streets were busy, and navigating through the crowds took most of our energy. We walked slowly, me limping, and the coffee and bagels were almost cool when we got back to the apartment with them.

"About last night..." I said in the kitchen.

"*Sleepless in Seattle*," she said, without looking at me.

"What?"

"I thought we were doing *Jeopardy*. 'I'll take romantic comedies for a hundred, Alex.'" As usual, she had recovered faster than me.

"Coming here was stupid, and it put you in danger and I don't know what the hell I was thinking of. I'm sorry."

"You did promise me an adventure," she said. "I would have been disappointed if I'd missed it." She unwrapped her bagel slowly, and took a sip of coffee. "There's one thing I didn't get a chance to tell you last night," she said. "I think I may have gotten a picture of the guy."

"So, that's what those flashes were! I thought I was having a religious experience."

She smiled and shook her head. "It was dark, and I didn't have time to set the camera or focus. I have no idea if they'll turn out."

"How long will they take to develop?"

"I'll do them right away, as soon as I get back to my place. I'll make sure you see them before I go." Her smile faded quickly.

"You don't have to go," I said. "You said last night you didn't want to."

"I also said I knew I had to." She took a small sip of coffee and then picked up her camera bag.

"I can't go with you unless you ask, you know."

"Yes," she said. "I know." I listened to her camera bag flap softly against the side of her leg as she walked out the door.

Six

I sat at the table for a while, working hard at not thinking about her, or about planes heading west carrying confused, thirtyish women with expensive matching luggage. I worked hard at not thinking about the corners of her mouth, about how we met, and about things she had said that made me laugh. I forced myself to think about wood and tools and screws and the physics of home security. After a while, I walked down those five worn, stained flights of stairs, out to the front of the building and sat on the front steps. To my surprise, there was still life in New York City. Traffic moved down 84th Street toward Columbus Avenue, across the bridge to Jersey, Route 80, the Midwest, and California. Or to the airport and then to London, Cairo, Tokyo, or Sydney. For all I know, some of those trucks may have been carrying supplies to Cape Canaveral, to be loaded on the space shuttle Discovery. Or, for all I know, to Mars or Jupiter, or the enormous stretch of dark space past Pluto where even the sun's light can't reach. After reading a James Joyce book in college, *Portrait of the Artist as a Young Man*, I think, I used to write my personalized cosmic address on the inside of my college notebooks.

Arthur McCullough
School of Business
NYU
New York City
New York State
USA
North America
Western Hemisphere
Earth
Solar System
Milky Way
Universe

Sitting on those steps in front of that crumbling building, I felt some small comfort in understanding my place in the larger scheme of things. My stupidity, my pain, my loneliness, would not have an effect on the unfolding of the universe. If it suddenly began to rain purple frogs, or if buildings grew lips and began to giggle, it would not be my fault. There was a certain safety in my insignificance, but I still hurt like hell. I went for a long ride in the subway. It seemed like the most comforting thing to do. It was still early in the afternoon, and the station was empty and quiet, just the way I like it. I let two trains go by, and then got on a downtown local. I had no destination. I just needed to move. I took the local to 42nd Street, and switched for the IND out to Queens. Queens had no particular appeal, it was just far. At the end of the line, 179th Street, I climbed up the stairs, crossed to the other side of the platform, and headed back to Manhattan. I tried to think about Jonesy, but for some reason I couldn't. I tried to think about the book, but couldn't. I could only think about me. My train of thought was ambling slowly through station after station, rolling on rusty wheels, and picking up no passengers.

I got back to Paulie's late in the afternoon, and called a building supply house in the Bronx I had done business with before. Yes, they had everything I needed, and yes, for an extra thirty bucks they would be sure to deliver it tomorrow morning. After a miserable dinner of leftover Chinese food and instant coffee, I resumed my cramped post in Mr. Rupert's bedroom. It was an uneventful night, and I managed to catch a few hours' sleep. I was on the front steps by 9:30, stretching and rubbing my sore toe, when the delivery truck showed up. I managed to drag two sheets of plywood, a couple of two by fours, screws, nails, and assorted hardware up those five flights. I rested for a while, and then covered each of the windows near the fire escape with three-quarter inch plywood, nailed and screwed to the frames. I nailed chocks to the floor and then braced the plywood against the chocks with the two by fours at a 45-degree angle from the floor. I installed another deadbolt lock and two slide bolts on the apartment door. A thief could still get in, but he would have to really want to, and he'd have to bring some serious tools.

As I was finishing up work on the locks, Mrs. Federico poked her head out of her door and called to me. "Yoo-hoo."

"Hello, Mrs. Federico," I mumbled.

"Oh, please call me Eugenia. And I haven't been a Mrs. in quite a few years."

"Well, okay then, Eugenia." Of the seven million people in New York, actually of the seven billion people on earth, she is the person I least felt like talking to at that moment.

"I've heard so much banging and hammering," she said. "What are you doing in there?"

"I'm putting in some new locks."

"Talk about locking the barn after the horse is gone."

"I suppose," I said.

"Would you like some company?" she asked.

"Well, I'm just about finished, and then I have to..."

"Oh, if you're finished, good, then it's a perfect time for a cup of tea."

I hesitated, trying to think of something else important I had to do.

"I could use the company," she said. "And I may be able to tell you something you don't know about Walter's book." That was certainly the right button to push.

I put the tools back in the kitchen drawer where I had found them and walked down the dim hallway to Mrs. Federico's. Her apartment was set up exactly as Paulie's: an entrance into the living room, kitchen and dining room area on the right, hallway to the bedrooms straight ahead. But her place was neater, cleaner and better maintained. There was new paint and a smell of furniture polish, wallpaper that didn't peel and faucets that didn't leak. We sat at a small, round breakfast table with a bright yellow tablecloth. She poured a cup of tea from a real china teapot, and frowned when I added milk to mine.

"I sent a friend to your apartment to meet you last night, Eugenia, and she knocked and rang your bell, but got no answer. Were you out?"

"Last night? No. I rarely go out. But I don't answer the door at night either. Besides, I didn't hear anything. There's all kind of noises outside at night, and I don't pay attention anymore."

"I guess it doesn't matter. You have a nice place here, Eugenia," I said.

"Yes," she said. "I'm one of the fortunate ones. My husband left me enough money to live on comfortably, and my son lives nearby, over in Throgsneck. He's such a help with shopping and repairs and what not. When he was little, he was such a—"

"You mentioned Mr. Rupert's book," I interrupted. The throbbing of a sore toe and my sore head were like a rim shot when she spoke.

"Yes," she said. "Yes, I did. He used to talk about it all the time. He was so awfully proud of it, and so upset that he had to sell it."

"Yes," I said. "I know it was extremely important to him. What did he tell you about it?"

"I'm not sure I should tell you. He was always so secretive, like it was life insurance or something."

"Yes, but Paulie thinks it might have something to do with his death. Any information you could give me would be helpful."

"Well, he did tell me...you will keep this in the strictest of confidence, won't you? It could be embarrassing to his family, even after all this time."

"The strictest of confidence," I said, crossing my heart. "I won't even tell Paulie unless I have to."

"He told me it was a code book," she said. "From World War One."

"A code book."

She nodded. "That's right. Walter's father had family in Germany, and they used to correspond, using the book as the translator. They would write innocent letters, and then put code numbers in invisible ink, like thirty-three, two. That meant the thirty-third word on the second page. Like that. Walter wouldn't tell me for sure, but I think they were spying on ship movements in and out of New York Harbor."

"German spies during World War One. That's really something," I said. "Tell me, do you read a lot, Mrs. Federico?"

"Yes, I do. I love novels, all kinds of novels. How did you know?"

"Just a wild guess. But even as a code book, I'm not sure why that would make it valuable today."

"Oh, it isn't really worth anything. My son told him so."

"Your son? Does he know something about books?"

"Oh, yes. Quite a lot. He buys and sells rare books, sort of as a hobby, sort of as a sideline. Walter showed it to him, and asked him to, you know, evaluate it."

"And what did your son say about it?"

"I don't remember exactly, but it made Walter very upset. James said Walter called him a nincompoop. No, it was more than that, a *twittering* nincompoop."

"Walter had a flair for the language, didn't he?"

"He certainly did let people know what he was thinking."

"Did you ever actually see the book, Mrs. Federico? I know Walter kept it hidden, but did he trust you enough to show it to you?"

"Oh, sure, he trusted me. We were very close for a while. You know, around the time we were dating and he asked me to marry him. He told me he thought we could have a wonderful life together. But, being Walter, he became angry and quite rude after I turned him down. Ha. After what I knew about him. Did you know…"

"Well, what can you tell me about the book?"

"Oh, I'm sure my memory wouldn't do it justice. But my son can certainly tell you what you need to know."

"How can I get in touch with your son? James, is it?"

"Yes, James, but I'm not sure you'll be able to reach him now. He is a very busy man. A teacher, you know, and of course, his side business with books. He should be a college professor, but he says he prefers to shape and influence the younger minds. The leaders of tomorrow, so to speak."

"Well, where does he teach? Maybe I can just have a few minutes of his time for a phone call."

"I don't think school is in session right now. I think last time I spoke to him he was talking about taking his family for a vacation. Camping, I think. Maybe I can let you know when he gets back."

It was late September. All the shapers and influencers of young minds had been back in the classroom for a few weeks now.

"Can I get you some more tea? Maybe something to eat with it?"

The mug I was drinking my tea from had a decal from DeWitt Clinton High School. "He doesn't by chance teach at DeWitt Clinton, does he?" I asked, holding up the mug.

She hesitated for a moment, mouth open. "No. Not anymore. He left there a few years ago because of some scandal among the faculty. I'm too much of a lady to even describe the goings on over there."

"I see," I said. "So where does he teach now?"

"I would rather let him talk to you. I'll have him phone you when he gets back. I promise. How about some toast?"

I had a sudden, brief memory of Mrs. Federico looking nervous, and switching a crumpled blue cloth from one hand to the other. "You know I was looking around for the green bag Walter used to keep the book in. I saw it on his dresser the other day, but yesterday it wasn't among all the wood. I wonder if the thief took it. I wonder why anyone would bother, if it was empty."

She cleared her throat and wrung her hands together. "Oh, the *blue* bag. I don't think it's green."

"It's just a little thing I can't explain. I mean why that blue, oh, yeah, right it was blue, bag is missing. You were in the room when Paulie collapsed. Did you see it in there?"

"Um, no. I was so upset about Mr. Dwyer, I didn't notice much. And I didn't actually go into the room."

"I guess someone could have taken it as sort of a souvenir or memento. I'll get in touch with that police officer...maybe he took it."

"Yes, perhaps he took it as a souvenir, or maybe evidence?"

"Is there anything you want to tell me, Eugenia? I mean as a detective working this case and searching for any clues, even small ones, that might help?"

"No. I really don't know what you are referring to, and I'm beginning to resent your tone."

I thought for a moment about pushing this envelope, and decided there were other things I needed to do. After turning down another piece of cinnamon toast, I promised to come back one day soon for dinner, and escaped to Paulie's apartment. The secretary at DeWitt Clinton confirmed they had a history teacher by that name, and I left a message asking for him to call me back.

I called the Metro Hospital and they told me Mr. Dwyer was permitted to have visitors, so I took the bus cross-town and walked, actually limped, the dozen blocks to the hospital. I hesitated at the door of Paulie's room, imagining him pale and in pain, hooked up to tubes and beeping monitors, but I had underestimated him again. He was propped up comfortably with just a blood pressure cuff and a single intravenous tube attached to his arm.

"Arthur," he said, in a voice strong enough to surprise me.

"How are you feeling?" I asked.

"I feel pretty good," he said with a broad smile. "In fact, I feel better than I have in some time. I've gotten two wonderful nights' sleep, and the food is actually not bad. I should have come to this hotel years ago."

He did look much better. His hair was trimmed and combed, and his face had color.

"I'm sorry if I scared you," he said. "It was weak and foolish of me to collapse that way."

"No, Paulie, no. No one can blame you for being frightened. Someone broke into your apartment and searched through everything in that room. That's pretty scary."

"That wasn't it, though, Arthur. That's not really what scared me. When I saw everything all over the floor in Walter's room, I didn't think a burglar did it. You'll laugh at me, but I thought it was

Walter's ghost, come back for his book. *That's* what scared me. I thought Walter had come back."

"Well, it wasn't a ghost, Paulie. Walter's or anyone else's. It was a flesh and blood human being."

"I know. A ghost might come back and search for something, but he would never hit someone on the head with a crowbar."

"How did you know about that?"

"Your girlfriend came to see me earlier today. She told me all about it."

"You're kidding me. Jonesy came to visit you? Here?"

"Yes. She wanted to photograph me."

"Are you sure it was Jonesy? She didn't tell me she was coming."

"I'm sure it was her. We had quite a long conversation after she took her pictures. She knew things about you no one else could know. She told me you acted like a hero the other night, trying to catch the thief, and she said you believe everything I said about the book." He was beaming at me, almost laughing.

"Yeah, I guess I do. I can't see any other reason to do what he did in your apartment, and I can't believe he came back again for a third time."

"If it's a he."

"Yeah, if it's a he."

"She's very pretty, you know. Really something special."

"The thief?"

He laughed. Actually laughed. "No, your girlfriend. How would I know what the thief looks like?"

A nurse came in, ignored me completely, checked his pulse, checked his blood pressure and fiddled with the intravenous pump.

"How's he doing?" I asked.

She finished writing something on a chart and then made eye contact for the briefest of moments. "Are you related to Mr. Dwyer?"

"No," I said. "I'm a friend. As far as I know, Mr. Dwyer has no relatives."

"Well, then, who takes care of him?"

"I take care of myself, nurse," Paulie answered.

She shook her head and didn't bother to look at either of us. "I'm not supposed to share information with non-family members, but you are apparently right that Mr. Dwyer has no family, so I'll bend the rules. In addition to his hypertension, Mr. Dwyer is anemic and seriously undernourished. His collapse and admission here may be the best thing that could have happened to him. However, I don't recommend passing out as a long-term medical strategy."

"When can I go home?" Paulie asked.

"Mr. Dwyer ought to stay here for at least a week," she said to me, or at least in my direction, "on intravenous hydration and a well-balanced diet, but his doctor tells me he is due to be released on Wednesday."

"Mr. Dwyer is glad to hear that," Paulie said. "He will be glad to get back home where, even if people try to scare you to death, at least they don't ignore you."

"Please have him fill out a dinner menu," she said to me and let the door close silently behind her.

We watched soap operas for a little while, Paulie flipping between two of them and explaining the plots of each.

"That one," he pointed to an on-screen redhead, "has been getting away with murder for years. Sometimes literally. She had an affair with her husband's brother and his attorney, both. Then she was convicted of hit and run, but she got out of jail on a technicality. She donates all of her husband's money to right-wing fascist organizations, and the poor snook still loves her." He flipped past a toothpaste ad, a talk show, and an infomercial for the latest fabulous home fitness machine, to the next soap.

"That guy with the crew cut is running from the Mafia. Married the daughter of the, what do you call him, the Don, and got caught cheating on her. How stupid is that? Like a death wish. The heavy woman with too much jewelry there is his neighbor, and she suspects his secret."

"Speaking of neighbors," I said. "I met Mrs. Federico."

"Oh, Eugenia. I hope I didn't scare her too badly. I went to her apartment after I called you. I didn't know where else to go."

"She was very upset over it, but by the time I left her, she seemed to have calmed down."

"She didn't tell you anything weird, did she?" He hit the mute button on the remote control. "These control things are great, aren't they?"

"Weird? Like how, weird?"

"Well, Eugenia says things. Things that aren't true. Walter used to think it was her medicine, but I think it may be some kind of a neurological problem."

"So, she tells lies."

"Whoppers. When we first met her, Walter and I, I guess we were still pretty naive." He leaned back and folded his arms carefully. "Not too hard to believe, two old men being fooled by a woman. Men are always suckers where women are concerned, but you probably know that already. Eugenia took us in completely, not once but twice. Right after she moved into the building, she told us she had just gotten out of prison. Served fifteen years for murdering her husband. He beat her and her children so severely, she told us, that she felt she had no choice. But while she was doing her sentence, even her children had abandoned her and she was alone and destitute. We believed it, of course. Who would make up a thing as terrible as that? After about six months, we learned it was all a big lie when her son and daughter-in-law started visiting her. Her son is a pretty straight arrow. John, I think."

"James, maybe?"

"Yes, that's it, James. He and his wife came to visit and we found out the truth. She had been ill for several years, in and out of an upstate treatment facility for severe depression.

"And god knows what else," I mumbled.

"When we confronted Eugenia, she broke down and admitted the truth, and then told us why she was depressed. She told us she had been Nelson Rockefeller's mistress for years, and when he died his family persecuted her. Soon after his funeral, she was evicted from her apartment, laid off from her job, and had all her savings and investments tied up in some kind of litigation. A whole government conspiracy. She said she went from a penthouse apartment to a woman's shelter in a matter of months. She could really tell a story, Arthur. She had me crying, and she actually had Walter choking up. When we asked how she happened to meet Mr. Rockefeller, she said they met through Richard Nixon, an old Army buddy of her brother's. I found out a year or so later that Nixon had served in the Navy."

"Wow, Eugenia, you go, girl."

"The most wonderful thing about her is she doesn't plan any of these fantasies. They seem to come spontaneously as she needs them."

I started to wonder if I were investigating a murder at the Algonquin. Everybody involved was a storyteller. "So, Walter didn't kill his wife?" I asked.

"No, he didn't."

"And you never threatened to throw him out a window?"

That one caught him by surprise. "Certainly not."

"So, probably, Walter's father wasn't a German spy during World War One."

He laughed. "What do you think?"

"I think perhaps Eugenia hasn't lost any of her skill."

More TV, which reminded me that life can be perfect if I would just smile more. And then even more commercials that reminded me why I keep my TV in the closet.

"Why didn't you tell me her son had seen the book? Actually evaluated it?" I asked.

"Oh," he said. "I was trying to convince you that it was valuable. Hearing what James said about it would not have helped. And I was a little worried about you hearing more whoppers from Eugenia. I'm sorry, Arthur."

"Well, is there anything else? Any tiny little detail you may have left out?"

"No, oh wait, yes. Did I mention he kept the book in a blue pouch? I remembered the name. It was Royal Crown."

"Isn't that the name of a cola?"

He thought for a minute. "No, it's Crown Royal. It's scotch or bourbon or something, and the bag was for one of the smaller bottles."

He pressed the magic button and we watched beautiful, well-dressed people overacting in elegant settings for a few minutes more. On the half hour, when there was nothing to switch to but commercials, Paulie asked, "Do you have any idea who's doing this, Arthur? Are you making any progress at all?"

I shook my head. "I still don't have any idea where the book is, or why it's valuable."

"You don't look well," he said. "You look tired."

"I've been a little busy. I boarded up the bedroom windows and added some locks to your door to keep the Vikings out of the monastery."

"She wouldn't tell me what he did," Paulie said.

"Who wouldn't tell you what who did?" I asked.

"Your girlfriend. She wouldn't tell me what happened when he broke in while we were all at the funeral. When I saw everything moved around in Walter's room, I got so scared, and I'm afraid I don't remember. Did he destroy my apartment? Do you think he found the book? She would only tell me to ask you."

"He apparently came back to do some carpentry work."

"Carpentry? What are you talking about?"

"He didn't break a thing, except the window frame when he came in. He just took everything apart...the dresser, the headboard, all of it. And carefully. It was all disassembled, and stacked in neat piles. When he climbed back in the next night, I caught him taking the molding off the base of the walls. Carpentry."

He smiled at me again. "It's almost as if he were searching for something small, say the size of a book."

"Yes," I said with my hands held up in the air. "I'm convinced. I am a true believer in the existence and value of Mr. Rupert's book, as least in the mind of this guy. And the fact he came back means he hasn't found it yet. That's the good news. The bad news is it probably isn't safe for you to go home. Is there anywhere else you can stay?"

"Oh, yes. I didn't think of that."

I suddenly realized my loft might be his best choice.

"I don't have a lot of friends left, Arthur. And many of them don't have places of their own."

"What about down the hall with Mrs. Federico?"

"Oh, I'm not sure she would have me right now. And I'm not sure I could deal with all of her storytelling, either."

"How about Walter's daughter? Do you think Marguerite would let you stay with her for a few days? Just until I can get this figured out."

He got a dreamy, distant look on his face, which I took to be a yes. I used his room phone to call Mrs. Emerson, and then let Paulie talk to her. After a stumbling description of his predicament, he asked and, with some back and forth, she apparently said yes. He held his hand over the mouthpiece and asked me if I could drive him out there.

"To New Jersey?" I asked. Why was everyone suddenly going west?

"Yes. New Jersey. That's where she lives. Can you drive me out there?"

"I guess I can rent a car," I said. "You get an address and ask if I can have a little time to talk to her about her father."

I arranged to rent a car and pick him up at the hospital at discharge time on Wednesday. When I left him, he was smiling. "That little Peggy," he said to me. "She's always been so good to me."

~ * ~

It was late afternoon and all of my clocks, internal and external, were whispering that it was time to go home. I hugged Paulie before I left. I didn't think about it, I just did it. My toe was really barking at me, so I took a cab home, elevated and iced it, and slept through the night. I heard the sambuca calling once or twice, but resisted.

Paulie was safe in the hospital, his apartment was buttoned up as well as I could button it, and Jonesy's flight was in two days. She would be two thousand forty-seven miles away. I knew that because the next day I bought a U.S. map, figured out the scale, and measured from Manhattan to Billings. 'Two thousand miles away' would be a familiar phrase running through my head over the next few days.

Shoved halfway into my mailbox that morning was a manila envelope with two photographs in it, and a note in her perfect, ornate handwriting.

"These are poor quality blow-ups of the only things distinguishable. I did the best I could do. J."

Both 8x11 photographs were done in three colors. Dark gray, darker gray and black. The first one had the faint outline of what could have been part of a torso and an upraised arm. The other held more promise. It was clearly the dark outline of a foot, or shoe, or sneaker. Inside that shape there was a small, lighter outline of a flattened crescent, or scythe. Or boomerang. I knew I had seen that symbol before. I went to my closet and looked through my old sneakers until I found it. It was the 'swoosh,' the symbol of Nike footwear. That certainly narrowed things down. In a city of seven million people, probably only about half of them wear Nikes. I could stop worrying about the penny loafer crowd, the cowboy boot contingent, ballerinas, quadriplegics and paratroopers.

~ * ~

In the main room, the dust from the wall was still settling. The air looked clear, except in direct light, but it had a gritty, chalky taste to it. There was a layer of fine plaster silt on everything, even the parakeets, that had to be dealt with. I had been dreading this cleanup, that's why it took me so long to get to the wall. No matter how carefully I cleaned, I knew the stuff was still settling and I would have to do it all again in a few days. But it felt good now, almost like a ritual, carefully cleaning everything I owned. I washed all of my dishes, pots, pans and flatware, dried them and put them away. I washed the floor and wiped down the walls and cabinets and light fixtures of the kitchen. I vacuumed the main room twice, wiped down the walls and then vacuumed again. I vacuumed the furniture, washed the drapes and the bedclothes, and then the windows. By the time I collapsed into bed, I had touched just about everything I owned, and it was all mine again. Not ours, mine. And permanently.

~ * ~

I called James again and got him this time, and we made an appointment to meet the next day near his school. I took the train up to Van Cortland Park and walked over to a small diner just off Broadway. There were only four people in the place...two of them were women and the other looked like he was cutting school.

"Mr. McCullough?" a man called from the booth in the far corner. James was short, like his mother, and had gray, thinning hair with no sense of direction. He wore tortoiseshell glasses, and squinted through them, which made him look like he was always in a little bit of pain.

"Thank you for meeting me," I said.

"A pleasure," he said with a smile, "although this will have to be a short meeting. I only get half an hour for lunch." He was drinking tea and reading the classified section of *The Times*. "My mother told me about you. She said you were very kind to her the day her neighbor collapsed."

"Your mother has been very helpful to me, too. She told me Mr. Rupert asked you to appraise his book."

"It was actually her idea. Rupert had bragged about it so much, I think my mother thought I would be impressed. I wasn't. It was really a very ordinary book."

"Your mother didn't think it was ordinary. She has a very interesting theory about Mr. Rupert's book."

He gave me a look I could not interpret, but I knew I had stumbled onto something sensitive. "My mother has a lot of interesting theories, Mr. McCullough. But she's seventy-seven years old, and she's entitled to them." I didn't know where to go with that one, so I just left it alone.

"When did you see the book?" I asked. "When did she ask you to evaluate it?"

"I go to my mother's for supper on Tuesdays. It would have been two Tuesdays ago. That would have been in early September, probably right after Labor Day. On the following Tuesday, I told him it wasn't worth anything."

"I don't imagine he took the news too well."

"No, not well at all. At first he thought I was kidding him. He was so totally sure I was going to declare him a millionaire, I really had to convince him the book was worthless. Once he realized I was serious, he got angry and accused me of cheating him."

"Can you tell me what the book looked like? Size, shape, color? Was there anything noticeable or recognizable about it?"

He reached into the briefcase next to him and brought out a textbook. "It was about this size, what they call quarto. Roughly nine by twelve inches. The *Pilgrim's Progress* I saw was just a bit thicker than this history book, maybe two hundred-fifty pages or so."

"Thicker than that? What color?"

"It was a pale brown, almost a cream color."

"Cream colored. Are you sure about that?"

"Yes. It was only two weeks ago I saw it."

"Any marks on it?"

"There was a pretty good crease in the spine. If it had been a valuable book, that would have brought the price down a good deal."

"No stains or other marks?"

"Not that I can recall."

"Did he handle it carefully? Did he keep it wrapped up in a cloth or something?"

"No, it was just the book. And he handled it kind of casually, ham-handed, actually."

"Mr. Federico, your mother doesn't have the book. At least I'm pretty sure she doesn't. So, you don't have to protect her."

"I don't know what you mean. Of course she doesn't have the book. Why would she have it?"

"When her neighbor collapsed, she was in his apartment, and I think perhaps she took the little bag the book used to be kept in. But I'm pretty sure it was just the bag, and not the book. A little blue velvet sack. I saw that bag on Walter's dresser the first time I was in there, but not the second time, after everything had been deconstructed. Isn't that what you're worried about?"

"Deconstructed?

"Yes. Deconstructed."

He stared in his tea. "I won't admit anything to you, Mr. McCullough."

"Mr. Federico, please believe me, I am not with the police. I am about as much 'not with the police' as someone can be. I don't believe your mother did anything wrong, or that you did either. I'm just trying to figure out where this book is, and why someone thinks it is worth all this trouble."

"My mother is old, and she can be difficult, that's all I'll say."

"James, if I may, there may be some danger here. That apartment has been broken into three times. And I have come to believe Walter Rupert's death was not a suicide."

That pushed him back in his seat a little bit. "So, that wasn't just another story of my mother's?"

"It took me a while to get there, but I think Walter was murdered, and I think it has something to do with the book. Can you tell me anything about it? The real one."

He breathed heavily for a while, pushed the hair off his forehead and finished his tea.

"Okay, the whole story. He did ask me to look at it, and give him an opinion of its value. And it wasn't my mother's idea, it was his. We sat at Mom's kitchen table and I looked closely at it. Yes, he pulled it out of a blue velvet-looking bag, and handled it like it was something fragile. Mr. Rupert would not let me take it with me, so I just took notes. I told him I would do some research and get back to him in a few days. Which I did."

"I want to be sure we're talking about the same thing. The book Paulie described to me was maroon, perhaps a hundred and fifty pages, and had a stain at the top. Is that the same book?"

"Yes. Maroon, and octavo, meaning roughly six inches by nine inches. Published by a Brooklyn firm, Corbin and Son. And I do remember it had a stain on the front cover. My first impression was that would reduce its value. But I was wrong."

"Why wrong?"

"Because the book had no value. It was something you could find in a bargain bin in any dingy second-hand bookstore. If you paid ten dollars for it, you would have been overcharged."

"Did Walter give you any hints as to why he thought it was valuable?"

"No, not really. Only that it was a Civil War relic that had been in his family for several generations. He used the phrase 'handed down' several times, like it was a religious ceremony. I told him it is a classic book, which it is, and he should keep it as a cherished memento from his ancestors. That's when he got abusive. I guess I can't blame him. He was dead right. Cherished mementos don't pay for groceries."

"His roommate, Mr. Dwyer, is convinced someone is trying everything possible to get hold of that book. He thinks that's the reason for Mr. Rupert's death, and for the burglary the other day."

He nodded, pulled off his glasses and thought for a moment. He had the kind of eyebrows that come toward the middle, and then make a right angle turn downward when he frowns. "So that's why my mother has been on edge lately." He swished a little of his tea around in his cheek. "I checked that book through several sources, and even put ads in two magazines, without response. I'm not the world's foremost authority, Mr. McCullough, but I'm convinced that book isn't worth anything."

"He told his roommate he was offered five hundred for it."

"Five hundred? I'm sorry, that just doesn't make sense. I really can't imagine why."

"The offer was from someone at Grove Street Bookstore. Ever heard of them?"

"Sorry, no. There are too many to keep track of. Mom and Pop bookstores come and go, especially when they are up against giants like Barnes and Noble. But that book..."

"Yeah, I got the same story from another book dealer downtown. He was just a pop, though. I didn't see any mom." I got that look I'm so used to getting. It's a long stare with a small head movement to the side that says so much more than just 'huh?'.

"There is one interesting thing I did uncover in my research. About the publisher, Corbin."

"I'm desperate. Any information you have might help."

"There was a scandal early in the 1870s involving one of Corbin's relatives. A nephew, if I recall. It seems this guy was forging signatures onto Corbin and Son books to drive up the price. He actually was convicted of fraud."

"Whose signatures?"

"Just anyone famous at the time. You see, if a book was owned by someone famous, it increases the price. This fellow was especially adept at signing Herman Melville's name. Moby Dick was a big seller at the time."

"Were there any signatures on the book you saw?"

"No. None. No writing of any kind on it, which is not really all that uncommon."

"Another dead end, I guess. Well, thank you for leveling with me."

"I'm sorry for all of the, ah, confusion. But, well, my mother."

I nodded to the waitress for the check. "I was serious before, too, James. Someone is willing to go to great lengths for this book. It may be a good idea to get your mother away for a while. Maybe she should stay with you for a few days. I don't know how serious this guy is, so it may be a good idea for you to be careful, too."

"That would just about guarantee a divorce, Mr. McCullough. My wife has even more difficulty than I do in separating my mother's fantasies and reality."

"Well, just a thought. Keep it in mind."

I paid for his tea, and took a cab back to 84th Street. Usually, you can spend a few challenging minutes trying to pronounce the name on the hack license, but on this luckiest of lucky days, I read I was being chauffeured by Sterling Wingate III. I guess his dad's investment firm had no openings, so he was trying his hand at the taxicab game. I over-tipped him, just for the hell of it. We blue-blooded scions have to stick together.

~ * ~

"Mrs. Federico," I said when she answered her door. The television was on in the background and there was a smell of dinner cooking in the kitchen. "I think there's something you aren't telling me."

She peeked under the door chain at me. "Whatever do you mean? Aren't telling you about what?"

"I don't know," I said. "I just had a conversation with James and I have a feeling your son is protecting you. I think he thinks you may have Mr. Rupert's book. Do you?"

"No, I don't," she said.

"Well, the book Paulie saw and the book your son evaluated are very different. He compared it to a full-size history book, cream color. We both know it doesn't look like that. If you don't have the original, then maybe he does." I pulled out my investigator's license. "This means I'm a 'friend of the court,' and I have a responsibility to report all tampering with evidence or obstruction of justice. I'm afraid James may have to answer some questions to the police." After years of watching cop shows on TV, I could spout this balloon juice as well as anyone.

She undid the chain and let me step into the room. "James doesn't know anything. I had it," she said with a pout, "but it's gone. I took it from Walter's room, but I don't have it anymore. I threw it in the garbage."

"Well, they'll probably go easy on you," I said, "on account of your age. But I'm not so sure about James. Tampering with evidence, hindering an official investigation."

"What evidence? It was just a..."

"Just a what? What was it you took before they took Paulie to the hospital?"

"It was just lying there. It was just lying on top of the wood. They were all out in the other room taking care of him, and it was right on the pile. It wasn't the book; it was just the bag. The blue velvet bag Walter kept the book in. I took it to remember him. I didn't know it was evidence." Right. She was holding something in her hands and twisting it when I had gone in after Paulie collapsed.

"Where is it now?" I asked.

She shuffled into the bedroom and came back a moment later with the bag I had seen on Walter Rupert's dresser the first time I was there, but obviously not the second. It was a blue, velvety material, just big enough to hold a small book, and it had Crown Royal in gold letters on the side.

I looked at her sternly, as if she had to learn not to be naughty before she grew up. "You took this from Walter Rupert's room the day Paulie collapsed. Is that right?"

"Yes. I didn't think it was important."

I dug around inside. "And what was in the bag?"

"Nothing, it was empty. Please believe me, it was empty." Damn, no cryptic clues, no treasure map, not even a Kilroy.

"Are you telling me everything now? Absolutely everything?"

She took a deep breath. "There is one more thing, but I swear I don't know what it means. 'Coals to Newcastle'."

"I'm sorry, what?" I asked. "Close to what?"

"Coals. 'Coals to Newcastle.' That's the last thing Walter said to me. The last thing ever. I saw him going into his apartment on the day he was killed, and he was smiling and humming. I asked him what he was so happy about, and he said, 'Coals to Newcastle, Eugenia. I've just delivered a load of coals to Newcastle.' Oh, he could be a caution."

~ * ~

It was usually the highlight of my day, the thing I saved up for and postponed until I had the time to savor it, but not today. Today it was the last thing I wanted to do, and I did it quickly to get it over with. I called Jonesy.

"Thanks for the pictures," I said. "I'm not sure how much they'll help, but at least I know I wasn't hallucinating."

"Sure. No problem."

"Listen, I don't want my stupidity to be the last thing you remember about me. Can I see you again before you go? Just once. We can meet somewhere in public, so if there's a fight, it will just be the normal New York ambience, and not my fault."

"I still have packing to do. And I'm having dinner with my mother. I don't know if seeing you is a good idea. It's hard, you know. It's just hard."

"I'm not thinking of anything heavy duty, just, you know, hangin' out. Sort of like closure."

A long pause. I listened intently for sobs or deep sighs, but there was no sound until she said, "Closure. I guess."

We met at Bryant Park, a one square block of greenery right at 42nd Street and Fifth Avenue, roughly halfway between her place and mine. It was overcast, threatening rain, and breezy. Early autumn, and things were beginning to change.

We met after the lunch crowd had gone back to work, so there were just enough people flowing by to play the game. She wore jeans and green sneakers, a bulky purple sweater and a Yankees cap. She pulled off her sunglasses as she sat down next to me without a word.

"I was just thinking about Simon and Garfunkel," I said.

She looked at me strangely for a moment and then said, "Oh."

"I was hoping you'd remember."

She nodded. "Sure. First date. You were such a big spender. You brought me to a park and fed me knishes. And sang that song. The one about old friends sitting on a park bench."

"And you taught me how to play the game."

We sat quietly for a few minutes, each lost, I suppose, in the jumbled, biased, alternate reality that is memory. I tried very hard to think of something to say. Something helpful, something normal.

There was a walkway through the center of Bryant Park and for a few minutes we watched the usual suspects stroll by: dog walkers, mothers with small children, businessmen. You could see someone coming for fifty yards, so it was perfect to play our favorite game, 'Who Could Do Better.'

"Here comes a couple," I said. The girl was trim, pretty, taller than the boy, and wearing a black suit with a very red blouse. "She is a secretary for a law firm, and he is a college student majoring in either English literature or journalism. His ambition in life is to be a congressional aide, probably for a Democrat. He probably won't make it. He'll end up as manager of a Dollar Store somewhere in Delaware. So definitely, she could do better."

Jonesy laughed, almost. She studied them for a moment. The boy was squat, needed a shave and had a thicket of brown hair robins could live in.

"I must beg to differ," she said. "She is a bank teller. I mean look at those orthopedic shoes. Poor thing must be on her feet all day. He is just finishing up his master's degree in computer science and will soon be working for IBM. In six months, he'll be pulling down six figures and living *la vida loca*. So, no doubt in my mind, he could do better."

"Yeah, you got me on the shoes. One point for the girls' team."

After a quiet, uncomfortable few minutes, she spotted her couple.

He was lanky and stooped, fortyish with thinning hair and a poor excuse for a mustache. She was athletic looking, graceful, well-groomed and expensively dressed. He was talking rapidly, with emphatic gestures, and she was nodding slowly. She was walking quickly, easily, and he was struggling to keep up.

"She," Jonesy said, "is a dancer, with some experience on Broadway, and runs a small dance studio on the East Side. She has an opportunity to choreograph a revue for a dinner theater production in Branson, Missouri. She sees it as a big career move, but doesn't want to leave New York. He is a thoracic surgeon, born and raised in Iowa, who just left his wife to be with her, and is mad as hell she is thinking about leaving. It's a close call, but he could have done better."

"Why? Why him?"

"Because if you manage to find someone you can stand in this world, and he treats you good, then you're a damn fool to leave him." That took a minute or two to sink in.

"I see him as a museum archivist for the Brooklyn Museum of Art. He gave up smoking recently, but he has emphysema. He is worried about his job because he knows the State is cutting funding for the arts, and he's also worried about her because she's been having knee problems. He knows if she gets injured in Branson, it could end her career as a dancer. Another close call, but she could have done better."

"Why? Why her?"

"Because he isn't comfortable with her self-confidence, he worries too much about her, and he worries he doesn't have a secure place in her life."

Another minute of uncomfortable silence, and then she said, "You know I'm not someone that curses a lot, but sometimes it just seems right to say, 'oh, shit'."

She put her sunglasses back on and stood. There were no tears in her eyes. "Here is the best closure I can offer you, Bird. Arthur. We had good years. You could not have done better."

I watched her walk quickly away: green sneakers, blue jeans, purple sweater. And behind her a gray, gray sky.

~ * ~

On Wednesday morning, I helped Paulie survive the rigors of a hospital discharge, and we headed for the sovereign state of New Jersey in a rented Chevy Impala. I had packed a bag for him, and got an extra set of keys made. We took the George Washington Bridge across the River of Death, paid the toll at the Hill of Difficulty Plaza, and had coffee at the Slough of Despond rest area. He looked healthier than I could ever remember him, and he was talkative for a change. He talked a little about Walter, but mostly about himself when he was younger. He grew up in the city, just like I did. His father was a steamfitter, and I didn't have the heart to tell him I didn't know what a steamfitter was. He was a pretty wild kid, and said he survived his school years with only one arrest and no convictions. After high school, a friend of his mother's found him a job with the Transit Authority, and his wildness and youth gradually succumbed to responsibility, consistency and routine. He was married once, for about eighteen months, but the marriage was so unhappy that when she left him, he didn't even bother to look for her. "I wish I could give you some advice about women, Arthur, but for my sins, I never figured them out."

"What about Walter's wife?" I asked.

"Hanna? Why do you want to know?" he asked.

"I'm trying to find out everything I can about Walter so I can find his murderer."

"Hanna has been dead for, oh Lord, almost thirty-five years, Arthur. I don't think she's a suspect."

"How did she die?" Perseverance, even in the face of logic, is the hallmark of a good investigator.

He sighed heavily and thought for a moment. "I haven't thought about it for years, and it still causes pain. She was killed in a subway mugging. Some animal with no respect for human life grabbed her pocketbook and she wouldn't let go. Brave Hanna. Lion-hearted Hanna. They struggled and he stabbed her."

"Walter must have been distraught."

"He was crazy with grief for weeks. He blamed himself for a while, then he started to blame the rest of the world."

"Kind of a pattern with him, wasn't it, blaming the rest of the world?"

He gave me a hard look and sunk into a sulky silence. "He was a good man," he said at last. "He made as many mistakes as any man can make in eighty years, but he was a good man."

~ * ~

There are two things I like about New Jersey. They don't have a state song, and they have a lot of well-paved and well-maintained highways. Well, there's one other thing I like: if you manage to keep a few miles away from Newark, you can't smell it. We drove quietly for a while, reading road signs and wondering about where some of the towns got their names. We passed signs for the Oranges (West and South), Nutley, Teaneck, Ho-Ho-Kus, and Paterson.

Paulie said to me, "Lou Costello used to say he was born out West. West Paterson, New Jersey. You do remember them, Abbott and Costello, don't you?"

"Sure. Who's on first, what's on second, I don't know's on third. A classic."

"Yes, that's right. I guess your father did teach you some of the important things."

"That wasn't my father," I said. "That was Saturday morning television."

The four-lane interstate blended easily into a two-lane state road, and Paulie read me the directions in his soft, but no longer tremulous, voice. We took the left fork just past the Jiffy Lube, did a three-quarter turn at a traffic circle, and crept along in traffic down a main street in what I think was Lake Hopatcong. We followed the signs for Lakeside Village and soon were in the domain of European cars, manicured lawns, built-in swimming pools, and cul-de-sacs. We turned off Lakeside Avenue onto Lakehill Drive, past Lakeview Court, Mountain Lake Boulevard, Scenic Lake Road, and turned onto Lake Vista Lane.

"I wonder if there's a lake around here?" I said as we pulled up at 7 Lake Vista Lane. It was an imposing brick Tudor house with a circular driveway and a detached three-car garage set away from the house. There was a stockade fence hiding the view of the back, but I was certain there would be a patio, a barbecue big enough to roast a mastodon, and an in-ground swimming pool.

Mrs. Emerson was waving from the front door, looking overweight and suburban, but very glad to see us. Or, at least one of us. I helped Paulie out of the car and he almost ran to her. After they hugged, she offered me a handshake and another of her low-calorie smiles. The house was bright, spacious and well decorated. There was a fireplace in the living room, art hanging on the walls, deep pile carpeting, a broad staircase, a wall of potted plants, and very little evidence that any of it had ever been lived in.

She took us to a small room off the kitchen with a single bed, a dresser and a television. On the dresser was a bouquet of flowers with a card that said, 'Get well soon. P.'

"We've set you up in here, Paul," she said. "It's a bit cramped, but I thought it would be easier being downstairs."

"This will be wonderful, Marguerite, and I can't thank you enough for letting me stay." He was holding both of her hands, and clearly had no intention of letting them go.

"You have a beautiful home here, Mrs. Emerson," I said.

"My husband is an architect," she said. "He and his partner built about half of the sixty units here in Lakeside Village. This was the original model, and I think it's the nicest of them all."

"Your dad would be happy for you, living in this luxury," Paulie said.

After a long pause, one of the pregnant kind, she said, "Would you like something to eat or drink? You've had a long ride."

"A coffee would tide me over," I said.

"I wonder if I might just lie down for a while," Paulie said.

"Of course," she said. She turned on the TV and fluffed his pillow while I found my way to the kitchen and sat down.

"Can you get channel four out here?" I heard him ask.

"He must be exhausted after the trip," she said.

"Yes, and it's also time for *General Hospital*." I laughed.

Seven

We had coffee on the patio, watching the leaves fall gently into the green, brackish pool water. The pool cover was balled up at the back of the yard, anchored by a rake and a chlorine canister. The grass around the perimeter of the patio hadn't been mowed in a while. I wondered briefly if there was still a Mr. Emerson.

Someone called out, "Mrs. Emerson? Marguerite?" and a woman poked her head around the corner of the house.

"I'm sorry to interrupt..." she said, and then, "oh, I see you have company. I'll come back."

Marguerite's eyes widened for a moment at the sound and she looked quickly toward the garage. "It's okay, Burkie, you just startled me a bit. Come on in and sit."

I immediately recognized 'Burkie' as Marguerite's companion and hand-holder from the funeral. She was a tall, slightly stooped woman with salt-and-pepper hair that fell down over one eye. She smiled warmly at me and extended her hand.

"I don't think you met Mr. McCullough at the funeral ceremony," Marguerite said. "He's a friend of my uncle Paul, and he's helping me to clear up some of my father's affairs. Mr. McCullough, this is my neighbor, Sharon Burke."

"The mysterious detective," Burkie said.

"Not mysterious on purpose, Mrs. Burke, just an outsider trying to keep a low profile." She sat, saying she could only stay for a minute, and while we chatted, she was furtively looking around the patio, the backyard and peering into the house. I was going to ask her if she had lost something when I noticed both of them were looking over at the garage.

Burkie said, "I just came over to see if Phil was back yet. Robert mentioned they had a date for golf this weekend and asked me to remind him."

"No, he's not due home until tomorrow, but if I talk to him tonight, I'll remind him. I'll ask him to give Robert a call."

"Oh, that'll do it," Burkie said pleasantly and stood. "Well, I'll let you get back to it. Good luck to both of you with all the paperwork. I was executor for my great-aunt's estate, and it was a nightmare. I learned that joke about why lawyers are buried ten feet deep." She smiled and nodded at me. "Nice meeting you, Mr. McCullough."

She left, walking around the house in a way to make a complete circuit of it, and kept her head turned toward the garage.

Just before she was around the corner and out of sight, she looked over at me and nodded again, slowly. From where I sat, I could see her emerge and cross the street. She went down the driveway three houses down.

"Sort of a friend, sort of the neighborhood busybody," Marguerite said. I sipped my coffee.

"You mentioned the other day you had questions for me," she said, with another shallow smile that made me wonder if my shirt was on inside out.

"Yes," I said. "About your father and his book. Paulie feels strongly the *Pilgrim's Progress* may have been why he was killed, and I'm beginning to agree."

She breathed deeply and sighed. "That hardly seems likely, Mr. McCullough. It was never worth anything. And besides, my family has owned that book since, well, forever. Why would it suddenly become valuable now?"

"I don't know. That's why I'm here asking stupid questions. I don't know if Paulie mentioned to you that the thief came back again."

"The day Paul collapsed, you mean?"

"Yes, but another time after that. Later that same night, in fact. Both times he was systematically dismantling your father's bedroom, obviously looking for something small."

"He came back again?" she asked, and her face went white.

"Three break-ins within a week certainly make Paulie's story more credible. Is there anything you can tell me about the book?"

"I don't think I can be very helpful. I haven't seen Walter Rupert or that damned book in more than thirty years. And to be honest, it isn't easy to talk about him."

"And you don't have any idea why it was valuable? He never told you?"

"It wasn't valuable," she sighed patiently. "It was a just a magic charm in my family. A talisman. He had it, my grandfather had it, and my great-grandfather had it before him. I don't even know how many generations back. My family went through some hard times during those generations, Mr. McCullough. We were German immigrants living through two world wars. I'm sure you can see what that means. If it really was valuable, I'm sure it would have been sold long ago."

"Your father did try to sell it just before he died."

She shook her head. "Paul told me, but I have trouble believing that. That book was never about money to him. It was always about his precious heritage. He must have been in pretty bad shape if he tried to sell it, because that book represented his ancestors, his tradition, everything of importance to him. All the baggage he dumped on me when I was growing up."

"Do you know how it happened to come into your family? Or when? Did your grandfather ever talk about it?"

"I never met my grandfather. He died before I was born, and Walter never said, so I assume now he didn't know. It just always seemed to be there."

"Do you remember where he used to keep it?"

She smiled a little. "In the Crown Royal bag. It was a blue velvet bag with a drawstring and Crown Royal in gold letters. I think Crown Royal was a fancy scotch or whiskey. I think all Walter Rupert cared about was that it looked fancy enough for his precious book. He had the bag stapled to the back of one of his dresser drawers. He would pull it out two or three times a year, his birthday and Christmas especially, and tell my mother and me the two stories about it."

"What two stories?"

She hesitated for a moment, and I thought she was going to cry. I don't know what I would have done if she had. One tear might have done it for my career as a detective. She stiffened for a moment, but pulled it back together pretty quickly. I bravely sipped my coffee.

"It was Walter Rupert being melodramatic, and nostalgic too, I guess. We always did Christmas up right. Mom did the tree...no one else was allowed to touch it. He set up the crèche, the one he had carved himself, and I made the cookies. For some reason, it was always five dozen, like the number five dozen had some magical significance. Walter Rupert reveled in Christmas, of course. It was so full of tradition and heritage and ceremony. But when he told the book story, he was really at the top of his form."

She took a deep breath. "Well, it seems one Christmas night, when he was about ten, the Rupert family tree caught fire. There were no electric lights in those days, of course, but people hung real candles from the trees. Hard to believe now, but that's what they used to do. Anyway, before anyone could do anything about it, the top of the tree was ablaze. Everybody started running in all different directions, except for my grandfather. He ran to the big steamer trunk in his bedroom, pulled out a book wrapped in canvas, and gave it to his son. He told him to run outside with it 'and always protect it.' That was Walter, and Walter Rupert did what he was told. He ran out and across the street with the rest of the family just in time to see the flaming tree come crashing through the front window and land in the snow. My grandfather somehow picked up the tree and threw it out a window. The apartment was saved and nobody was hurt, but Walter never forgot that night."

"Quite a story," I said. "That would make a powerful impression on a ten-year-old boy." She had referred to Mr. Rupert as 'he,' 'him,' and 'Walter.' Never 'Dad' or 'Pop' or even 'my father.'

"Yeah. I used to love to hear it. Until I got sick of it, and him, I used to beg for him to tell it. Imagine that."

"What was the other story?"

"Oh, I couldn't even do that one justice. It was a deathbed scene. My grandfather knew he was dying, some kind of cancer, I think, and he made a big ceremony of giving the book to his son. And of course, Walter acted like he had been given charge of the crown jewels. That's where all his crap about heritage started, I think."

"I guess I'm beginning to understand why it was so important to him."

"Oh, it was important to him, all right. Just not to anyone else in the world. Beauty in the eye of one beholder doesn't necessarily translate into value."

"True enough," I said. "But whoever broke into his apartment three times thought it was valuable. Can you think of anyone else who might have known about it? Anyone else who may have wanted it? Cousins, aunts, uncles?"

"No. he was an only child, and all of his uncles and aunts were dead before I was born."

"Did you ever mention the book to anyone? A friend? Your husband, perhaps?"

"I was so glad to get away from Walter Rupert and his suffocating ways that I rarely talked about him to anyone. My husband never even met him."

"You mentioned at the funeral that you and he were estranged, but I'm not sure I really understand why. I'm sorry to pry, but, well, Paulie."

"Yes, I know Uncle Paul can be persistent. Toward the end, Walter and I fought all the time. Spiteful, hateful things we said to each other that, of course, I regret now. He had his obsession about tradition and heritage, and the way things ought to be. He felt anything new was bad, and he tried to hold my mother and me captive in the nineteenth century. We struggled against it, of course. Things like TV, radio, and air conditioning were all battlegrounds. 'This is not the way people should live,' he would scream at me. He actually got mad one time when I used the elevator."

She got up from her chair, and walked to the glass patio doors. She kept her back to me, but I could hear the trembling emotion in her voice. "The final battle was about a job and buying a car for my mother. After a two-year campaign, she finally got a job, but it was evenings, in Canarsie, almost an hour train ride. She was a saleswoman in a small dress shop, and she loved that job. He dug his heels in about the car and I never understood why. I still don't. We had the money to get one, then. But he wouldn't budge and Mom rode that goddamn train two hours a day until she was killed."

"Paulie told me she was mugged in the subway."

"Mugged, yes," she said bitterly, her voice and volume rising. "That's the euphemism people used then, too. My mother was a little more than 'mugged', Mr. McCullough. She was beaten unconscious and then stabbed eleven times. And why? Because she was riding the subway at eleven o'clock at night, instead of driving home from work in a car."

A long pause after that one. "That must have been an awful time for you."

"Yes, it was. I was only seventeen at the time, and a bit of a drama queen, I suppose. I thought of killing myself, but mostly I thought of killing my father, if you can imagine something so horrible. I thought of taking that goddamn book and choking him with it, or using it to set him on fire. I moved out a few months later."

"When was the last time you saw your father?"

"I haven't seen him or talked to him since the night he caught me stealing his book. But please don't get the idea I thought it was valuable. I just wanted so much to hurt him, to take something important away from him, like he took something important away from me. But he caught me. I had just gotten it from the pouch at the back of the dresser and was about to start ripping pages out of it. He grabbed it away and smacked me.

"'Someday this will be important to you'," he shouted. "Unbelievable. I had just lost my mother, and he was telling me about how something made of cardboard and paper was important. He was an arrogant, ignorant man, and I hated him for years." She turned to me for a moment, tears streaming down her face, and then disappeared into the house.

I felt drained and totally out of my element. Is this what detectives are supposed to do? It occurred to me to just quit. Tell Paulie I was done and find him someone else to do his taxes. But then I had the flash of Walter's body on the sidewalk. And another of the terror I saw that night in Jonesy's eyes, and I was angry.

I finished my coffee and then finished Mrs. Emerson's coffee, too. Not a stiff drink, but it would have to do. I went back inside to say goodbye to Paulie, but I was too late. He was sound asleep under an afghan, pointed in the general direction of the sacred realm of *General Hospital*.

Mrs. Emerson had pulled herself together and waved to me from the front door as I drove away. I wanted another conversation with Burkie before I tried to think seriously about any of this, but I didn't want Mrs. Emerson to know. I think Burkie didn't want Mrs. Emerson to know, either.

I drove around a few blocks, although nothing was square, so I'm not sure they were blocks, but found my way back to Lake Vista Lane, approaching it from the other direction. I parked about half a block away and sat for a few minutes trying to figure out what to say to Burkie. I was the only car on the street.

She opened the door as soon as I rang the bell. "Please come in. I'm glad you figured out my message."

"I just have to know, why *do* they bury lawyers ten feet deep?"

"Because down deep, they're not so bad," she said with a big smile. "I need to share something with you, but I'm afraid it isn't much."

"'Isn't much' seems to be my lot in life these days, Mrs. Burke. You seemed very nervous with Mrs. Emerson."

"Marguerite, yes. Not nervous, maybe, but curious. There is something fishy over there. Robert, that's my husband, doesn't play golf and Phil probably wouldn't play with him anyway. I haven't seen Phil in a couple weeks. I think he may have moved out."

She backed up into her living room and I followed onto a chair. "We aren't nosy people, Mr. McCullough, but it's a quiet neighborhood, and my picture window is pretty much pointed at their house. We saw, and heard, Phil tear out of the driveway, maybe ten days ago, like a bat out of hell, and we haven't seen his Caddy since. And one other funny thing...the garage. They were fixing up a room over the garage, but construction seems to have stopped. No more trucks, no more workmen, but I still see lights in there sometimes."

"Do you think maybe Phil is living in there?"

She just shrugged. "I don't know what to think, but she has not been herself lately. I thought it was her father's death, but I don't know. I'm tempted to look in the garage window, but that seems kind of creepy."

I couldn't think of any way this would connect to the book, so I gave her a business card and left. It was my tax accountant business card, but, oh well. I looked over my shoulder as I walked away. The Emerson house was quiet, and there was no movement in the garage. There was a police cruiser idling next to my car, and a cop in a brown uniform looking in the windows. Brown uniforms make me nervous. I think they're all from Alabama.

"That's my car, Officer. Is there a problem?"

He was young, with a narrow, smooth face, and hair just a little too long for a cop. He stepped back, stood straight, tucked his hands in his belt and took a long hard look at me.

"Are you a resident here in The Estates?" he asked.

"No. I just drove someone here to visit a friend of his. A Mrs. Emerson." I pointed to the house.

"Emerson. Phil Emerson," he said, more as a statement than a question.

"Yes. My friend is an old friend of Mrs. Emerson."

"Do you know Phil Emerson?" The thumbs came out of the belt.

"No, I don't. I just met Mrs. Emerson the other day, but my friend has known her for quite some time. Is there a problem?"

The officious functionary was suddenly gone, replaced by a civil servant going through his routine. The name Emerson seemed to be some kind of magic wand.

"Well, the community usually frowns on street parking, although there is no specific ordinance prohibiting it. Usually, the resident makes a call to the town clerk if they expect people to be parking in the street."

"I wasn't aware of that. I'll be more careful when I come back to pick up my friend."

He tipped his hat, actually tipped his brown policeman's hat, got into his car and drove away. That gave me a little more to think about. But later, the subconscious mind being the buried treasure that it is, I found myself humming the old Beatles tune, "Rocky Raccoon," but it still didn't quite click.

~ * ~

I slept badly that night, tossing and turning with nightmares I didn't remember the next morning, and felt cramped and cranky as I walked uptown to the Grove Street Bookstore. This time I found signs of life. A few tables full of coverless, secondhand books stood just outside the entrance, and a faded "OPEN" sign was hung on the front door. Inside it was dark, musty and overflowing with books. From where I entered, I could see nothing but books, a forest of books, stacked on shelves taller than I am, with narrow, shoulder-width aisles between them. About halfway down the center aisle, a youngish, blond man peered at me over the cash register. As I got closer to him, both the blondness and the youth faded. He stood at a small, neat and organized little desk squeezed between the dusty and crowded bookshelves.

"May I help you?" he asked flatly, without looking up at me.

"I understand you sell rare books here," I said. "First editions, things like that."

He nodded, still without looking up. "Uh-huh." His hands were in constant motion, arranging papers, sweeping crumbs off the counter, rearranging a pencil box. Up close, the appearance of youth completely dissolved. He was thin and muscular, but with deeply etched lines around his eyes and the corners of his mouth. His hair was a glossy silvery gold, much darker at the roots. He didn't seem to belong there, or anywhere else I'd ever been. He was an aging beach boy, lost in a literary forest.

"What particular rare book or first edition or thing like that are you interested in?" he said without expression.

"I'm looking for a first edition of Lawrence's *White Peacock*. Would you happen to have a copy?"

He picked up a small, stapled bundle of typewritten pages and started looking through it. "Lawrence is the last name, right?"

"Yes," I said. "D.H. Lawrence."

He looked carefully for a moment and said, "I don't see anything by anyone named Lawrence in our catalog. Let me check the shelves." Reluctantly, he sidled out from behind the desk and disappeared down another aisle. I walked around, looking in both directions down each aisle. In the far corner of the building, a half-open door led to a small apartment. I could see another man, his feet up on a stack of books, reading. He was a bulky man, with drooping jowls and shaggy hair that curled over his collar.

The beach boy re-appeared and said, "No. No *White Peacock*. We have several books by Lawrence, but no *White Peacock*. Is there something else you're interested in?"

"Well, I'm interested in collecting first edition books with birds in the title."

Without turning, he called to the other man. "Mr. Kale, there's someone here interested in a first edition. Can you help him?"

I heard a grunt and then some vaguely friendly noises and the overweight and unhealthy-looking man strolled toward us. His jowls and his stomach quivered slightly with each step. "My name is Lloyd Kale," he said with a smile and an outstretched hand. "I am the owner of this establishment, and I would be happy to answer your questions."

"I was hoping to find a first edition of Lawrence's *White Peacock*, but you don't seem to have one."

"Edmund, have you checked our inventory?"

Edmund just looked at him with a blank expression.

"You are a collector?" Kale said to me.

"It's an interest I've just acquired. I would like to start building a collection of first editions."

"A worthy enterprise. Book collecting can bring a lifetime of enjoyment. But how did you come to be interested in *White Peacock*? There are so many good firsts that could begin your collection."

"I'm interested in books with the names of birds in the title."

"Oh, I see," he said. I was sure he didn't. No one ever does.

"Maybe you can just help me out with some information," I said. "I don't really know much about book collecting. I'm just getting interested in it, really. I have a lot of trouble judging the value of a book."

The bleach boy yawned. "I usually just look at the price tag."

"Edmund," the big man snapped. "I've warned you about your sarcasm before."

Edmund sneered at him for a moment, then turned quickly and disappeared behind a bookshelf.

"I apologize for my associate," the man said. "He is somewhat new to this business, and hasn't yet developed a passion for literature. Books don't make you smarter, but if you have some native intelligence," he looked toward where his associate had disappeared, "they can broaden it. I don't have the exact quote, but that is a sentiment expressed by John Harrington, said to be the inventor of the flush toilet during the reign of Queen Elizabeth the first." He said this with the air of an actor delivering Hamlet's soliloquy to a packed house. He paused for a moment, and I think I was supposed to either clap or ask for an autograph.

"But to answer your question. Value, like beauty, is in the eye of the beholder, especially in a literary commodity. If one thinks of value in terms of money, there are several surface artifacts which alter the meaning of a book's, shall we say, cash translation. Age and condition are the most obvious, of course, but often the least important. The number of copies in a printing, especially if the book turns out to be popular and long lasting and only a few copies were made in, for example, the first printing."

"You mean first edition."

"Yes. And often there are factors which relate to the history of the book. That is, who printed it and under what circumstances, who owned it and happened to write his name in it. A good example is the Bay Psalm Book. It was printed in 1640, a relatively recent vintage to a real book collector's palate. It was certainly not a first edition of the Book of Psalms. It wasn't even especially well printed, well-illustrated or expensively bound. In the scheme of things, quite an ordinary volume. And yet, it sold at auction recently for about fourteen million dollars, simply because of its history. You see, it was printed by the Pilgrims twenty years after their landing at Plymouth Rock and it's the oldest book printed in what has since become the United States. Had the British won the Revolutionary War, it would have been as worthless as a cookbook."

"Cookbooks aren't valuable?"

"Oh, they certainly can be. I have seen some go for two or three thousand dollars. But in your case," he continued, "esthetics determine value. Esthete, by the way, in Greek, means one who perceives. It is your perception that books with birds in the title are valuable. Who can argue?"

"You mean like the song, 'One Man's Ceiling is Another Man's Floor'?"

"Precisely. What a marvelous quote. I collect books of quotations myself. That sounds like a Dorothy Parker. Or perhaps a Groucho Marx."

"No, Paul Simon. The singer, not the senator."

He looked deflated, but only for a moment. "Yes. Of course. At any rate, I'm confident I can find a copy of this *White Peacock* for you if you'll permit me to serve as your agent."

"I might be willing to do that," I said.

"Or perhaps you would like to look around for another book to begin your collection." He handed me a fresh copy of the catalog. "We may have something in here with a bird in the title."

"A friend of mine referred me here." I pulled the Grove Street business card out of my pocket. "A Mr. Rupert."

"The name is not familiar," he said.

"He was in here just a few days ago with a copy of *Pilgrim's Progress* to sell. He told me you made him an offer."

"I do seem to remember someone, an older gentleman I believe, came in here with a copy of *Pilgrim's Progress*. Let me check." He took a small notebook from under the counter. "Yes. Here it is. It was a W. Rupert. William, I think."

"Walter, actually."

"Yes, Walter, of course. I did at least get his first initial right. Walter Rupert. I remember telling him I could get a good price for the book. The binding was in such good condition for an antebellum edition.

"Antebellum?"

"Yes. Antebellum. It refers to something printed pre-civil war."

"I know what antebellum means. I'm just surprised Walter had a book that old."

"You said the book was *Pilgrim's Progress*. Yes, I think it was. I haven't heard from the gentleman, so I assume he decided to keep it."

"Last I heard he was waiting for the value to appreciate."

"Ah, well, if he should change his mind, I'm certain I can find a buyer for his book. And yes, for that particular book, I think it could go as high as five hundred. As for you, sir, if you would like to look around, please feel free."

He walked me around to a section in the back where all the first editions were kept. "We have a full shelf of 'firsts' here, and there are always more on the way. Please feel free to browse. In the meantime, I'll do a search for the *White Peacock* you asked about."

I browsed, skimmed, opened, flipped, and otherwise killed time until he came back. "I've located a dealer in the Baltimore area with a *White Peacock* first edition to sell. He's asking seventy-five dollars for a copy in mint condition. I think it's a good price, and might be exactly what you're looking for."

"Seventy-five."

"Yes. Actual cost to you would be $86.75, including my fee."

"Oh, of course. That's a little more than I wanted to spend."

"Well, think it over," he said, smiling like a used car salesman. "You already have one of my cards. Call me if you're interested. And please give my regards to your friend. Tell him my offer still stands."

"I'll do that," I said. He walked to the back of the store again, bouncing, like a lot of big men, on the balls of his feet. I looked around for a while, marveling at the diversity of old, boring books people would pay a lot of money for. A few of them were stories that had been made into bad movies, and the rest I'd never heard of. I saw Edmund, the bleach blond associate, at the end of the aisle, pulling books off the shelf and wiping them with a cloth. He did everything quickly, ballistically, compulsively. He glanced over at me once or twice from the corner of his eye, but seemed to be too busy, or too surly, to take much notice of me.

There was no *Pilgrim's Progress* and nothing by John Bunyan. I stared at book titles for a few minutes, hoping for inspiration, and then left. Ignorance did not feel at all like bliss.

I picked up some cold cuts, macaroni salad and a six-pack of beer on the way home. After I'd eaten, I sat at my computer to organize what I knew so far. Using an electronic file card program, I started cataloging my acquired information.

STACK 1: THE BOOK

I could discount James Federico's bogus description of it, considering that his mother was actually the fabulous Mrs. Baron von Munchhausen. So, *Pilgrim's Progress* by John Bunyan: maroon, stain on the front cover, published by Corbin & Son, a Brooklyn company who had an autograph scam going on way back in the nineteenth century. Hidden by the Rupert family for generations, and no one knows why. No one knows why it is valuable. And no one believes it is valuable except Walter, and the windbag at Grove Street Bookstore.

And he knew Walter. At first, he said he didn't remember him, but then he did.

STACK 2: PEOPLE

Mr. Rupert: obviously not the sweet old character I thought he was. Obsessed with heritage. Became arrogant. Alienated his family. Got into an argument with 'P' before he died.

Paulie: lived with a cranky old man in a crumbling apartment for decades. Had opportunity to kill Walter but probably not the strength or the will. According to Mrs. Federico, an unreliable source at best, he had a motive. Had opportunity to search his bedroom. Inherits everything from him, including the book. He's a suspect, I guess, but not a very good one.

Mrs. Emerson: hated her father, hasn't seen or talked to him in years. Tried once to destroy the book. Knew where it used to be hidden. Married to an architect who seems to have some juice in northwestern New Jersey.

The thief: came three times and never got past Mr. Rupert's room. He (she?) has some inside information. Probably wears Nike sneakers. Owns a crowbar and used to own a flashlight. Knew Paulie's name.

Booksellers: All of them remember Mr. Rupert, except the people at Grove Street Bookstore. All of them told him it was worthless, except Grove Street Bookstore.

STACK 3: THINGS

The mess: What other reason is there for carefully disassembling a room than to search for something small? And all of Mr. Rupert's books had the covers taken off.

Rupert's journal: The bookstore that showed interest but was "playing it cute," was definitely the Grove Street, but who was the 'P' for whom heritage suddenly became important? Was it Paulie? No, he wasn't part of the Rupert heritage. Marguerite told me she hadn't been in contact with her father in thirty years. I wondered if she had any children. I looked up and noticed that I had typed Paulie as 'Pulie.' I backspaced to fix it until I got to just the letter 'P.' I remembered the card attached to the flowers on the dresser in Mrs. Emerson's spare room. 'Get well soon, P.' Her name was Mrs. Emerson, but called herself Marguerite, and everyone knew her as Peggy. Not exactly Lennon and McCartney, but I got the gist. It didn't rhyme, but this time the message came through.

She had to be the 'P' that called and talked to her father about tradition. I wondered what else she was lying about.

STACK 4: EVENTS

The murder: why murder him at all, and in such a gruesome way? Why not just knock him out, or tie him up or stuff him in a closet? Why was Mr. Rupert killed?

The break-ins: how did the thief know no one would be home? Okay, the funeral, but how did he know to search only in the bedroom?

STACK 5: SQUARE PEGS/ROUND HOLES

What was that purloined/sirloined all about? Why did Walter have a cookbook in his room if he never cooked? Did he actually say 'Coals to Newcastle,' or was that just another monkey wrench Mrs. Federico was casually tossing into my already sputtering machinery?

Sherlock had his seven percent solution, Nero Wolf had his beer, Hercule had his little gray cells. All I had was a very neat concept map connecting all the facts. I had all the suspects together in a virtual living room, but I still had no idea what the hell was going on.

~ * ~

I read a book once, something about Zen and fixing motorcycles, that said the state of 'stuckness' is a good place to be, because the thinker has lost his pre-conceived notions. From there, all solutions are possible...it's just a matter of choosing the right one.

In that case, I was in a perfect position, because I was as stuck as stuck could be. No one knew anything about the book, no one believed it was worth killing for, the police believed Walter Rupert killed himself. And I had no Jonesy to talk it over with. All I did have, looking at my mind map, were two references I couldn't connect to anything else. Purloined, meaning stolen, and 'Coals to Newcastle,' meaning taking something to where there were a lot of those somethings. So, Walter, being shifty, stole something and hid it in plain sight. No...he didn't steal something. That son of a gun, he brought it with him. *Huh*, I thought, *a clue.*

I have a light in my bedroom set to turn off at exactly eleven-thirty to remind me it's bedtime. The light over my head turned off at exactly the moment the lightbulb over my head went on.

~ * ~

I called the Grove Street Bookstore next morning, a little surprised they had a working phone, agreed to the $86.75 price for a first edition *White Peacock*, and asked how soon could I get it. Kale was sorry, actually, 'deeply contrite' that his business worked on a cash only basis, payable prior to his exertions. Could I bring a check around?

So I slept late, drank too much coffee, and walked to the Grove Street Bookstore, Est. 1931. The clerk, Edmund, apparently had some kind of religious experience, or perhaps a change of meds, because he greeted me with a big hello and a polite smile. "I'll get Mr. Kale for you. He's just in the back."

There was a small desk in the back corner with a little more light than the rest of the store, where Kale and I exchange checks and receipts. Edmund disappeared, but poked his head around the corner twice to study me. It seemed like a lot of attention for an $86.75 transaction. The Betty Crocker cookbook on Rupert's bookshelf was still an outlier, and I hoped, a clue. I asked Kale if he carried cookbooks. "Recently divorced," I told him.

"Well, you have my sincere condolences or my hearty congratulations, depending on the circumstances. Certainly we, Edmund and I, don't know you well enough to decide between the two, but perhaps, if you do come to embrace the charms of book collecting, we may in the future."

As it happened, the cookbooks were on the same bookshelf, just a few rows down from the first editions. The distinctive green plaid of the Betty Crocker that had been on Rupert's night table caught my attention at just below knee level. This one had the cover still on. On my hunch, I opened to a page about in the middle, and instead of finding a recipe for meatloaf with carrot garnish, I entered the further adventures of Christian as he is descending into the Valley of Humiliation. I checked to see if my two new friends were peeking and then I slipped the paper cover off. The hardcover book inside was a faded maroon color with a red stain at the top, and said *Pilgrim's Progress* in faded gold letters right in the middle.

"Jesus," I said. I thought of tucking it in my pocket and just walking out, but twelve years of Catholic education wouldn't allow me to commit even this small, justifiable larceny. I carefully put the book back inside its cover and walked to the counter.

There was no one at the desk. Kale was nowhere in sight, and Edmund was busy placing books on a shelf near the front door.

"I think I'll just take this for now," I called. As he turned to walk toward me, I noticed he was wearing dark blue Nikes.

"Did you find everything you were looking for?" he asked politely.

"Yes," I said. "I think I did. Your stock here is marvelously eclectic."

"Eclectic? Well, yes. I suppose it is, if eclectic means what I think it means." He took the book and looked it over for a price tag.

"Two ninety-five," I said pointing to the price penciled in at the top corner. "The value of the book is right there on the price tag, just like you said."

His smile slipped a bit, but he ignored the jab. He wiped the book off with a cloth, but didn't open it. He put it in a small bag, rung it up and gave me my change, still smiling.

"Thank you for your patronage," he said. "I hope we see you here again."

And just like that, I walked out of the store with the elusive *Pilgrim's Progress.*

~ * ~

I looked closely at it as I walked south on Broadway, turning each page slowly, looking for something out of the ordinary, feeling the binding and the covers for anything unusual, anything that could be a clue. It was not a thing of beauty.

> *The Pilgrim's Progress*
> *From This World To That Which Is To Come*
> *Delivered Under The Similitude Of A Dream*
> *Wherein Is Discovered,*
> *The Manner Of His Getting Out*
> *His Dangerous Journey And Safe*
> *Arrival At The Desired Country*

Catchy title, but a little too much for *The Times' Sunday Book Review*. The cover was a faded maroon, like Paulie remembered and James Federico lied about, and the pages were dried and yellowed. There was a stain on the top that seeped through about an eighth of an inch on most of the pages. There were no markings on it of any kind, nothing written on the inside blank pages, and nothing written in the margins. It was just an old copy of a bad book. If it had any value, esthetic or concrete, I couldn't see it. I couldn't see why someone would pay two ninety-five for it, much less kill a man, scare another into the hospital, and burglarize an apartment three times.

'Purloined.' That's what Mr. Rupert said, and that's what he did. I had to admire the old guy. He had hidden the book in the most obvious place imaginable. On a shelf in a bookstore. Who would think of looking for it there? Not me. Well, not for a while, anyway.

But why? Why hide it at all? It had been safely hidden in his room for thirty or forty years. Why move it? Obviously because someone knew where it was hidden, and only someone close to him could know that.

~ * ~

I spent the next morning at the library again, reading through books and journals on collecting books, acting like I knew what I was looking for. After three hours, I had found no reference to a Corbin & Son edition of *Pilgrim's Progress*. Not even a reference to the scam James had told me about. In desperation, I went back downtown to the Sage Bookstore, and talked to the owner again. He was behind the counter this time and the young assistant was moving things around on a shelf.

"I found it," I said to Bernard Prowse.

He looked at me through red-rimmed, bleary eyes.

"You're supposed to say, 'Eureka!'" he said.

"I'm supposed to what?" I noticed he was swaying a little bit and his head was not too stable on his neck.

"Eureka! That's what civilized people say when they announce a great find. Eureka! It's Greek. I don't know how to say 'what the hell are you talking about' in Greek, but if I did, now would be the right time to say it."

"Oh, sorry. I was in here the other day asking about a book. A copy of *Pilgrim's Progress* a friend of mine was trying to sell."

He stared at me for a long minute, and looked over at the young man working at the shelves. "Oh, right. The old guy. Worthless book. Called me a commie, or some damn thing."

"Yes, that's the guy. I found the book." I handed it to him.

He sighed. "Yep," he said, carefully paging through *Pilgrim's Progress*, "this is the book the old gentleman brought in, but it's no more valuable now than it was then." He closed it firmly and handed it back to me. "What do you want from me?"

"It's a long story. Will you give me enough time to tell it?"

He breathed some alcohol fumes on me. "Slow day, I'm bored. I'll stop you when it gets too maudlin."

I told him about the break-ins, the body lying on the concrete, the condition of Mr. Rupert's bedroom, and especially about the separation of books and book covers. "I'm convinced this book has some value for someone," I told him. "Is there any explanation, even a fantastic one, that could explain why someone would want this so badly?"

He ruminated for a long minute. "There are a couple of foolproof techniques for verification I've read about," he said. "The first involves a chemical solution that, when poured on the pages, somehow indicates age and whether they have been erased and written on before. In the

Middle Ages, they did a lot of that to save writing material. Called it palimpsest. The problem is the chemical solution may ruin the page."

"Ah," I said.

"Well spoken," he said. "The second technique involves, I think it is UV light, or gamma radiation or something. I get all that science stuff confused. But again, it can indicate, not a certainty, but an indication, what has been written on a page before."

"Wow," I said.

"Again, astute," he mumbled. While he was saying all of this, he was thumbing through the book, one page at a time, and paying more attention to it than to me.

"The third, and last one I can tell you about, is something Isaac Newton was experimenting with. He thought if you focus on a page with light that has passed through a prism, it can then be chopped up and used as a basic ingredient in alchemy. It can turn paper into gold."

I got it then. "I see. You are yanking my chain."

"Yes, yanking for all I'm worth. Sir, please get it straight, this book is not worth anything. *Anything.* I do feel bad about your friend, but he was just as much in error as..." He stopped and looked carefully down at the book.

"Okay, I get it. You can stop yanking now. I'll just go."

He frowned and shook his head, and gave me an exasperated look. He kept pinching with the front and back pages.

"There's no writing on the inside leaves, front or back," he mumbled. "That's kind of unusual. People like to own this kind of crap.

"They're different," he said to me. "The front page is thicker than any of the other pages. Double thick, like two pages were, oh boy, stuck together." He bent the bottom of the front page back and forth a few times. "I felt something. Derek," he called to one of his clerks, "put a kettle of water on."

"Not for me, thanks," I said. "I had coffee on the way over."

"Obviously it didn't help much." He continued to poke and prod the first page until steam was coming out of the kettle on the little hot plate near the counter. He brought the book over and held the page in the steam for a few seconds. He pinched the edge of the page between his thumb and forefinger and bent it back and forth until small white flakes fell from the page.

"Glue?" he said, mostly to himself. "What the hell have we got here?"

He steamed it again, and more of the white flakes fell. He bent the page back and forth carefully until it separated and he could slip a coffee stirrer between the two pages. He sawed carefully with the stirrer until the two pages were open, and we could see a faded inscription on the inside page, just barely legible:

Mr. President:
The way to heaven lies through the gates of hell,
Cheer up, hold out, with thee it shall go well..."
signed, W.W.

He sat down quickly. "I will be goddamned." he whispered to me, blowing another smell of whiskey much too strong for eleven o'clock in the morning. "I will truly be goddamned."

"What," I said. "What is it?"

"I don't even want to say it out loud. It's too wild."

"Oh," I said. "You're yanking my chain again."

"No, sir. I am not. If this is what I think it is, you will soon be able to hire a small regiment of lawyers to protect your chain from ever being yanked again."

"You're serious? You've found something."

"Right now, it is only a maybe. But an intriguing maybe. There is a story, a legend actually, about Lincoln and a book that figured in... no, I'd better not say."

"Say what? Figured in what?"

"I really don't want to get your hopes up," he said. "It's such a long shot it's ludicrous."

"But you said 'maybe'."

"What did you say your friend's name was? The old guy that owned this book."

"Walter Rupert."

"Okay. One cranky old bastard to another. For Walter Rupert's sake, I'll say maybe."

~ * ~

After carefully making photo copies of the inscription and taking a half-dozen Polaroids of the book, he promised he would make some calls and see what else he could find out about the legend.

I kept the book. It didn't fit in my shirt pocket, the back pocket didn't feel secure, holding it in my hand felt too exposed, so I jammed it into my front pants pocket.

I went for another long ride in the subway. I didn't think I had enough to go back to the police with. Not yet. I didn't think I had enough even to go to Paulie with. Even with the book wrapped in a plastic bag and stuffed in my pocket, I was no closer to figuring the why or who of Mr. Rupert's murder. The only thing that stood out from all of this was the fact that the book was hidden at Grove St., and that the people at the Grove Street Bookstore were the only ones to show the slightest interest in the book. It just convinced me I needed to pay a lot more attention to the denizens of the Grove Street Bookstore, Est. 1931.

I had been stumbling around the edge of this thing, whatever it was, hoping it would go away. Hoping, I hate to admit, that Walter really was a suicide and I could get back to my life. But now it was time for the detective to do some detecting. I reached back into memory for all the stuff I had read to get my investigator's license, and started to make some plans.

Eight

The next afternoon, I leased a car from Rent-a-Wreck, an old Buick Skylark I thought would look inconspicuous. By six the next morning, I was parked on Grove Street, about half a block from the bookstore, with a good view of the front door. I stretched out as best I could and pulled my Blue Jays cap down low. Around nine, Edmund unlocked the front gate, dragged out the two tables of discount books, spat, gave the whole world a defiant scowl, and went back in. Around 11:30, Kale came out, walked down Grove toward 14th St. and out of my sight. He came back about 15 minutes later carrying two brown paper bags, presumably their lunch. I took the opportunity to run to a coffee shop and grab some lunch of my own. Well, I didn't run, actually. After five and a half hours in a car, the best I could manage was a spirited hobble. The afternoon was almost as lively as the morning. During the course of the business day, only about a dozen people entered the shop, and only half of them came out carrying a book. Not exactly Macy's on Black Friday.

The lights of the store went out a little after eight, and half an hour later, Edmund pulled the sale tables into the store and dragged a pair of beat-up metal garbage cans to the front curb. I waited for another hour, until Grove Street was dark and deserted. I put on my rubber gloves, left the car quietly, and walked to the front of the building. I could see a dim light coming from the back of the store. I pulled the lid off one of the cans and yanked out the green baggy. Thank God someone in there was neat enough to use a plastic bag. I tossed the baggy into the trunk of the Skylark and drove home. Well, almost home. I had to park about 10 blocks away and walk back to my loft carrying a full bag of someone else's garbage. Mom and Dad would have been so proud.

In the main room of my loft, I spread out a drop cloth, put the rubber gloves back on, and started picking through Edmund and Kale's garbage. Yuck.

It was only about half as disgusting as I thought it would be. There were bread crusts and coffee grinds and pieces of putrid meat with unidentifiable things stuck to them, but a lot of the trash seemed to be carefully and neatly packaged. A lot of the paper products—tissues, napkins, receipts and scrap paper—were folded into neat triangles or rectangles and placed into other containers. Small boxes full of paper and cardboard were fitted into other boxes. Almost anything that could serve as a container did actually contain something. I started shoveling the runny, disgusting stuff back into the garbage bag, including a mousetrap, complete with mouse, and then pulled apart all the containers. There were cereal boxes folded neatly inside other cereal boxes, grocery lists folded into perfect squares, a tissue box torn at the corners, and flattened to a rectangle.

Newspapers were carefully folded to fit into the boxes. More of the messy stuff...ends of bread, cereal, fruit, was stuffed into milk cartons. One of these people threw away his garbage, and the other one packaged it. Going carefully through the boxes, I found a receipt from a grocery store with a phone number scribbled on the back. Finally, something that looked like a clue. I shouted 'Eureka' and thought of Bernard Prowse.

I poked and prodded, unwrapped and unfolded for a while longer, until just about everything was back in the garbage bag, and then I dragged the bag outside, washed my hands twice, showered, and washed them again. The day wasn't a total waste of time. I learned that both of them lived behind the bookstore, that at least one of them was compulsively neat, that they had mice, and that they didn't bother to recycle. It wasn't worthy of the Nobel Prize for detecting, but it was something.

~ * ~

My answering machine had a message from Jonesy, "Hi," she said in a flat voice. "Call me."

I tapped number one on the speed dial and she answered on the second ring. "I wasn't sure I would talk to you before you left," I said. Ah, hope springs eternal in the human breast.

"I finished up my packing and I remembered some things I left at your place. There's some stuff to give back to you, too."

"Okay," I said. "I'll come over. What do you need?"

She gave me a list that included some jewelry, shoes, sunglasses, and makeup that had accumulated here over the past few years. "No problem," I said. "I'll scoop everything into a box and be over in a few minutes."

"Bird," she said. And then silence. It wasn't the familiar silence that told me more than I wanted to know and then shut me up. This silence was not something she controlled, but something controlling her. "I went to visit your friend Paulie the other day," she said, finally.

"Yeah. He told me. That was a surprise."

Another silence. "I wanted to meet him," she said, "to try to learn something. You don't know it, but you two share a secret."

"What secret?" I asked, totally lost.

"Doesn't matter. He couldn't really tell me the answer anyway. But at least I got his picture. He has a great face."

"I'll bet no one's said that to him in a while."

"Well," she said.

"Well...I'll be over in a little while with your stuff."

"I'm on the way out to visit my mother. How about just leaving it with the doorman. I don't trust him, but he's scared of my mother. Long story."

"Okay." I wanted to say something supportive, something mainstream, silent majority, heartland, middle America. I wanted to show her I was really a sensitive, new-age kind of guy who was in touch with his feelings, but not so self-absorbed as to take her for granted. But I didn't. Before I could think of anything, she hung up. On TV when someone hangs up on you, there's a click and then a dial tone. In real life, here in the Valley of Despair, there is only a hollow, bottomless, electronic emptiness, and the distance between two electrons or two galaxies. In cyberspace, no one can hear you moan.

~ * ~

At 7:30 the next morning, I was back on the beat at Grove Street, yawning and bored, but better prepared than yesterday. I brought sunglasses, extra food, a book on tape, and an industrial drum-sized thermos of coffee. Using the cell phone I had picked up from Jonesy's last night, I tried calling the number I had pulled from the garbage in all the local area codes. In (212) I got a hair dresser, in (718) a coffee shop, in (203), Connecticut, the number was no longer in service and in (201), Jersey, I got only silence, probably from a dead cell phone. Finally, I tried it as an (800) number, and a woman with a head cold answered, "*American Bookman Magazine.* Classified department." There didn't seem to be anything sinister or meaningful about an antique book dealer having the number of a magazine about antique books. But wouldn't the number be in a Rolodex or an address book, rather than on the back of a receipt? Unless perhaps it didn't belong to the book dealer, but the book dealer's assistant. That was worth a phone call to *American Bookman Magazine.*

"Yes, hello," I said, ad-libbing, and trying to sound both sincere and intelligent. I can usually manage only one at a time. "I'm hoping you can help me. I'm trying to locate a book offered by a customer, and I believe he placed an ad in your magazine not too long ago."

"Yes," she said, and coughed. It was a deep, nasty bark.

"Is there any way you can trace an ad for a specific book?"

She sighed, and barked again. "Yes. We keep extensive digital records of our ads, by date, by book title and by name of the subscriber."

"Oh, that would be great."

"Well, that is, if you are a subscriber to our magazine."

"Oh, well, I'm not currently, but I have been planning to sign up with you for some time. I do much of my work through the *Bibliognost*, but I have found your publication to be of superior quality."

We made arrangements for me to subscribe, the rate was surprisingly high, but I said I would get a check in the mail the next day. "But I am in kind of a tight spot, time wise, about this book. It's kind of an embarrassing story."

"What's the problem?"

"Well, this is really embarrassing, but I wrote down the name of the book he was offering, and I lost the note. I don't remember what he was trying to sell and I promised him a quick answer. I feel like such a dope. I'm hoping you can let me have the name right away. It would really help me out. It would be an ad from a Mister Kale, representing the Grove Street Bookstore. If memory serves, it would have been early September. He was somewhat desperate."

"Oh, sir. I really don't think I can do that. You really need to have a—"

She started to cough again, and this one evolved into a genuine hacking fit.

"Have you ever tried blackberry brandy?" I asked.

"I'm sorry, what? What do you mean? Is that the name of a book?"

"No, no, I'm sorry, I kind of switched topics there. Your cough, I meant. I had a bad cough like that last spring, and someone, probably a bartender, suggested blackberry brandy was a good home remedy. I bought a pint, wrapped myself up in a warm blanket and sweated it out. Within twenty-four hours, I was soaking wet, but not coughing at all. I was amazed. Maybe you should try it."

"I could get in trouble. Not with the brandy, with the subscription."

"Yeah, okay. I don't want to get you in trouble. Forget it, I was just taking a shot. I'll put a check in the mail tomorrow and you'll notify me when the subscription is activated, right?"

A little cough this time, fully under control. "Why don't you give me your address, and I'll see if I can help you. And a phone number where you can be reached. And just so you're aware, we sometimes work through a collection agency staffed by people with no sense of humor."

I gave her that information, and she put me on hold to look up the ad. "It was not the name you asked about," she said eventually, "but a Mister Federico placing an ad in reference to a book titled *Pilgrim's Progress*. I would guess it's something about Thanksgiving."

"Thanksgiving, yes. *Pilgrim's Progress*, of course, for James Federico. But nothing for Kale?"

"Well, yes, here it is. Another ad referring to that same book, back in July. That one came from the Grove Street Bookstore, but no name. The caller referred to it as a 'book emporium,' which generally indicates it's a small operation with delusions of grandeur."

"Grove Street. Yes, that's the one. Well, thank you very much for that information." That was good news/bad news. It was confirmation that the Grove Street Grenadiers were interested in the book, but it made me wonder if they knew of James Federico's interest. "You won't forget to send in the check, will you?"

"I will not, I promise. And you remember to try blackberry brandy. And wrap yourself up good."

~ * ~

The street scene outside the Grove Street Bookstore was pretty much a replay of the day before. Edmund opened the gates at just before nine, and spat on the sidewalk, just to give me that *déjà vu* feeling, I suppose. Lots of people passed by, very few of them went in, and most of those that did came out again empty-handed. It wouldn't take a Dun & Bradstreet report to see this business was in trouble. My eighty-six bucks must have seemed like sudden wealth to them.

Around noon Edmund left for lunch, and I quickly got out of the car to follow. He strolled casually until he was out of view of the bookstore and then began to walk briskly, walking about as fast as he could without running. Between his yellow t-shirt and his silvery blond hair, he was pretty easy to keep an eye on, even from a distance, and to follow, even with my cramped legs. The streets were busy enough to keep me hidden, but not so busy I couldn't keep him in sight. Staying to his left and about a hundred feet behind, I could see his yellow shirt bobbing up and down with just my peripheral vision. I kept my head down and matched his pace, keeping him in the corner of my eye.

He stopped long enough to buy two hot dogs and a soda, and gulped them down quickly as he walked. He went east on 14th Street, and then turned north at Sixth Avenue. He went into the post office on Sixth and 16th St., and I trotted to catch up with him. I put my sunglasses on and pulled the bill of my Blue Jays cap down. It was lunchtime, so fairly crowded, and nervously I slipped inside. I spotted him right away, angrily banging shut one of the smaller post office boxes. I managed to skirt around the edge of the room and keep behind him as he locked the box and walked out of the building. I checked the number of the box: 277058. I didn't want to take the chance of following him again, so I hung around the post office for a few minutes, and then snuck out.

I took the long way around to get back to Grove Street, being careful not to accidentally bump into Edmund on his way back to work. I went north, stopped at the Muhlenberg Library on 23rd Street, and found the two latest copies of *American Bookman*. In the classified section, where I hadn't bothered to look before, there were seven or eight pages of small, two-line ads. On the fourth page I searched, I found it:

> Have 1861 Corbin & Son Pilgrim's Progress
> Historical Value Intact Reply PO Box 277058

I checked through the previous month's issue, and found the same ad. Edmund and Kale had been advertising the book since July, two months before Walter Rupert even decided to sell it. In a September issue, with a different post office box number, I found the ad from James Federico.

I made a big detour to get back to Grove Street, and expected to find at least one parking ticket on the windshield, but there weren't any. I stopped at home, then made a quick stop at the safety deposit box of my bank with the book. I put another small but powerful item in the box too, just in case. It was something no private investigator worth his salt would be without in this dangerous day and age. A cell phone, with 911 programmed in.

It was around four o'clock when I got home. I didn't know what to do with myself. I had firmly established, at least in my own mind, that the Grove Street Grenadiers had something to do with both the murder and the burglaries, but I had no idea what to do next. Jonesy was probably in the air by now, or in Montana tiptoeing around cow patties. Chasko would be no help. Kale and Edmund were busy not selling books. Paulie was probably half-asleep watching *As All My Children Turn In Dallas General Hospital.*

I called James at the high school and left a message. I gave him my home number, as my cell phone would be assigned another mission, and asked him to please call this evening. "This is not business as usual, Mr. Federico. I am concerned about your safety and perhaps that of your mother. I don't have enough information to go to the police, but I think you should be very careful. Please call me and I'll explain."

I fed the birds and cleaned out their cage, played about half of "Fly Me To The Moon" on the sax, and started taking measurements for my next project, the basketball court with a parquet floor. I had the dimensions marked out, roughly a thirty-by-thirty-foot half-court, and was trying to figure how far out from the wall the backboard should be when I made another of those decisions that wasn't a decision. I seem to have one of those brains that travels on two tracks at once, when it travels at all. When I'm focused on one thing, I'm able to make up my mind about another. As a freshman in college, I was in the middle of a sentence in *Jaws* when I decided to major in accounting. On my hands and knees in the main room, with a tape measure in one hand and a parquet tile in the other, I realized I would just have to force Messrs. Kale and whatever the hell Edmund's last name was, to commit themselves.

~ * ~

In my office under the bedroom, I sat with a pad and pencil and made up a script. I was afraid I would be too nervous to remember what to say. I draped a handkerchief over the microphone section of the phone and dialed the number on the crumpled business card.

"Grove Street Bookstore," Kale answered.

Good. You're the one I want first. "I'm reading an inscription from a small, maroon, Corbin edition of a really horrible old book. The inscription is signed W.W. Any idea who that could be?"

There was a long silence on the line. "Who is this?" he asked finally.

"John Bunyan," I said.

"Whoever you are, you have my attention."

"That wasn't from memory," I said. "I'm reading from the inside cover of the genuine article."

Another long pause. "I would very much like to see the genuine article."

"I'm sure you would, considering how much time and trouble you've gone through to get it. Be at the Grand Central concourse at ten tomorrow morning. Wait for me under the big American flag," I said, still reading from the script and struggling to keep the tremor out of my voice. "And don't bring your lap dog."

"How will I recognize you?" he asked.

"You won't need to," I said. "Just park yourself under that flag and I'll find you." I had a little trouble hanging the phone up.

~ * ~

That evening, I called James Federico again and this time I got him. "James, this is Arthur McCullough. We met the other day at the diner. I mentioned there may be some element of danger in all of this, and a phone conversation today reinforced that fear. The people I suspect are involved may be aware you placed an ad for *Pilgrim's Progress* in *American Bookman*."

"Placing an ad is just a legitimate...oh, I see. They may see me as a path to finding the book. But, sir, the book, as I explained, is..." he stopped, and there was an awkward silence.

"James?"

"Have you seen these people? Can you describe them to me?" he asked.

"One is easy to describe. He is large and overweight and has a perpetually happy face. He looks a little like Sidney Greenstreet, but probably more like Alfred Hitchcock if someone had told either or them a joke."

"And the other?"

"A little harder to type. I would say mid-thirties, maybe five foot ten, athletic looking, silvery hair combed pretty much straight back. No facial hair. Casual clothes, jeans and sneakers. Oh, and he seems nervous all the time. Pretty much in constant motion."

"Tan? Sort of a surfer boy look?"

"I'm afraid so. You've seen him?"

"Outside my mother's building last Tuesday. He was leaning on a lamppost, like a B-movie bad guy is supposed to. And he was there when I left, as well. He followed me to the subway, I think, and then I didn't see him anymore."

"Have you spoken to your mother lately?"

"Yes, today, in fact. She's fine, as always."

"Well, I only know that his name is Edmund, that he and the overweight guy work in the Grove Street Bookstore, and that one of them put an ad a few weeks ago describing a Corbin and Son edition of *Pilgrim's Progress* with historical value intact."

"That they had it to sell?"

"Yes. And we both know they didn't. That's suspicious. I'm not paranoid, James, and not normally an alarmist. I don't know what is going on here, but I believe these men are worth being concerned about."

"What are you suggesting?"

"If you have any sick time, or even if you don't, take a vacation. Go somewhere with your family, and even take your mother along."

"That's, um..."

"The better part of valor, James. I know you don't know me, and I agree this sounds like a subplot from a bad movie, but I keep picturing Walter sprawled out on the sidewalk. You should, too."

"How about going to the police? Oh, never mind. What would we tell them?"

"I am working on something that will let me bring the cops into this, but it will take a few days."

A long silence, punctuated by a couple of 'Dads' in the background.

"I have a sister out on Long Island. Maybe we can camp out in her back yard."

"Good, that will work. And as soon as I know something, I'll let you know. You have my home number. Please just keep your eyes open."

"Yeah, I will. And thank you."

~ * ~

The main concourse of Grand Central Station is a wide-open space roughly twice the size of a football field. From it you can connect to the subway, buses, taxis, and airport limos, just in case I needed to get away in a hurry. It was the perfect spot for the conversation I had in mind. It's almost always busy, but it's also so big it never seems crowded. I would be able to observe Kale, and talk to him, but keep my distance and never be alone with him.

During the year and a half I worked for an accounting firm on 43rd Street, I spent a lot of quality time walking through the shops and leafing through the magazines at the big newsstand, so I knew the layout pretty well. I waited on the steps of the east balcony where I had a good view of the whole concourse, and could watch to be sure Kale had come alone.

Kale arrived a few minutes early and stood looking uncomfortable and out of place among the business people and commuters streaming past him. I waited a full ten minutes, nervously fingering the record button on the tape recorder in my pocket, before I was satisfied he was alone. I came up behind him and switched on the tape recorder.

Short sentences, I told myself. *No facial expression. Maintain eye contact. Do not let him know how nervous you are.*

"So good of you to come," I said.

He turned quickly and smiled at me. "It occurred to me it might be you," he said. "I thought you were smarter than you looked."

"I suppose there's a compliment in there somewhere," I said.

"No, not really," Kale said. "Simply an honest observation."

"I have a feeling there's very little about you that's either simple or honest," I said.

"Ha! An excellent riposte. I assume we are here for a business meeting."

"Of sorts. I want to know who killed Walter Rupert."

"I don't know what…you mean the old gentleman who brought the book in?" He did look genuinely surprised.

"Nice job. Have you had dramatic training, or is lying a natural skill?"

He took a moment to gather himself, but his expression didn't change. "I assure you, sir, I was unaware he had died. And I fear now you are going to tell me it had something to do with the book he tried to sell."

"A fair assumption."

"Can I ask how he died, without seeming callous or disingenuous? I was truly unaware…"

"Very good," I said, starting to get a little angry. "Very Sidney Greenstreet. He was thrown off a fire escape."

Kale made the right moves. He looked down at the ground for a few moments and sighed deeply. "I am very sorry to hear that. But I did not harm the old man, nor did I wish him any harm. My only interest was in an honest commercial transaction. I wanted to purchase his book."

"Right," I said. "For the binding, which was in such fine condition for an antebellum edition. Antebellum meaning before the Civil War."

He smiled. "Yes. I will plead guilty to being somewhat duplicitous, but that's the nature of the rare book business. In fact, it's the nature of most businesses. I make no excuses and I beg no one's pardon for what I offered Mr. Rupert."

"And yet soon after that offer, which he refused, he was killed."

"Those two facts, harsh as they appear, may not be connected. Again, I offer no excuses or explanations, I only want to know more about what you read to me over the telephone."

"I want to believe it wasn't you who actually killed the old man," I said.

"It certainly was not, but I don't have the wherewithal to prove it. Today is the first time I have heard of it, and I can only assume it was some kind of an accident."

"Being dragged through a bedroom window and lifted over the railing of a fire escape doesn't meet my definition of an accident."

That did catch him off guard, like he honestly didn't know how it happened. "My colleague is an adult, at least in the chronological sense of that term. But I will allow that he has more than his natural share of unalloyed stupidity."

"I'm sure there is a statute that attempts to distinguish stupidity from homicide."

I scored a hit with that one. "It's my hope we can avoid any entanglement with statutes. Did you happen to bring the book?"

I shook my head. "This is only a preliminary meeting, Mr. Kale. To outline our respective positions, set terms, and if all goes well, schedule another meeting."

"You do seem to be in control of the situation."

"Yes," I said. "I am."

"What is it you want, Mister...?"

"Only two things. I want the murderer of Mr. Rupert, and I want a fair price for the book."

He laughed. "I'm not sure I can give you the first, and I'm sure I don't know the second. Besides which, you're being unreasonable. The death of your friend may well have been an accident and unconnected to our transaction, and is a *fait accompli*. We cannot change it. We are, however, at a juncture where careful negotiation can make us both very wealthy. Shouldn't that be your prime concern?"

"Call me old-fashioned. Throwing an old man off a five-story building offends me."

He smiled at me. "I am as appalled at violence as it seems you are, sir, but I bear no responsibility here. All of this is totally outside my purview."

"I think it was Perry Mason that said 'lack of remorse is the number one reason juries bring in the death penalty'."

Kale sighed. "I don't have a way to bring your friend back, but if you do really have the book, I believe I can certainly make your grief much more comfortable."

"If I really have the book? You mean the small maroon Corbin and Son edition of *Pilgrim's Progress* with the brownish stain on the top of the pages? The one published in 1861 with a charming but cryptic inscription on the inside cover? That book?"

"Yes," he said slowly. "That one. You do seem have me at a tremendous disadvantage."

"I want to know what happened that night, and I want whoever killed Walter Rupert in jail. If it was your associate, fine. Give him up to the police, and you can walk away scot-free. And then we can discuss the book."

He had a thoughtful moment staring at his shoes. "I'm not sure I can arrange that for you. Edmund and I have a little bit of history together. It might not be prudent of me to discuss his, shall we say, character flaws, to the local police. He can easily turn vindictive."

"We appear to have a standoff, then. I still have what you want, and you still have what I want."

"That may not be quite accurate," he said slowly. "You have something we both want, but you seem unwilling to negotiate openly. Why should I believe you would sell it to me when I give you what you want? And since my hands are not entirely clean in this matter, it could be several years before I was at liberty to enjoy the fruits of our bargain. This is not acceptable. And by the way, I think there may be one other element to the equation we haven't discussed. Knowledge. I know why that book is worth all of this turmoil, and just how to cash in on it. I don't think you do. You should not be so certain of victory, as I have not lost the game yet. I still have moveable pieces on the board, so I think we will be talking again." He bowed slightly with a little smirk and walked away, eyeing me over his shoulder.

As soon as he was out of sight, I went outside to an umbrella vendor and got a hot dog and a soda. Being terrified always makes me hungry. Fortified, I found a quiet phone booth and called Grove Street Bookstore again and read my second script.

"Hello," Edmund answered.

"Are you aware that at this moment your boss is making a deal that gets him the book he wants so badly and sends you to jail for murder?"

"Who is this?"

"Just a pilgrim trying to make some progress," I said. "If you want to discuss a way out of this mess, meet me at noon at the corner of Varick and West Broadway. Keep it to yourself, though. Three's a crowd." I hung up the phone and remembered to breathe.

This was the scary one. I wasn't sure he would come, and I was half hoping he wouldn't. I chose that particular corner because it was close enough to Grove Street for him to sneak away, and it was just across the street from a police station. The Seventh Precinct station was a huge, imposing, Greek-looking building with blue and white squad cars parked outside and cops coming and going in all directions. I didn't think Edmund could be stupid enough to try anything there, no matter how much I prodded him. It was a busy enough street to catch a cab uptown, too. If I could get something definite on Edmund, I could hand deliver it to Chasko in less than twenty minutes.

I got there about fifteen minutes early and waited. I had plenty of time to wonder just exactly why I was there, waiting calmly for someone who was probably a killer.

I spotted Edmund coming about half a block away and stood in the middle of the sidewalk, repeating my mantra: *No facial expression. Maintain eye contact. Don't let him know how nervous you are.* I pushed the record button on the tape recorder again. When he got near, I held up my hand and said, "Edmund."

It took a moment for him to recognize me. "I thought it might be you." he said, "What's this all about?"

"Pretty much what your boss said. I guess I didn't fool anyone."

"My boss? I don't have a boss. I have a partner."

"I didn't get that impression during my extended conversation with him."

He looked toward the police station nervously. "Can we go somewhere, in a shop or something?"

I ignored him. If he was nervous, maybe he wouldn't see that I was, too. "I had an interesting discussion with Mr. Kale earlier today. He told me he would trade you for the book."

"Trade me? What are you talking about? What book? What is this?" He was in constant motion as we talked. Nothing overt, but fidgety, small, controlled movements: stroking his cheek, rubbing his hands together, flexing his shoulders, like a third base coach giving signals. I wondered if he was high on something. I really thought people stopped doing that stuff years ago. After the first moment he saw me, he didn't make eye contact. He looked around at everything else with equal interest, or lack of interest, and I had no more appeal than a traffic light.

"Oh," I said. "You're looking for some orientation, and perhaps some identification. The book in question is an 1861 Corbin and Son edition of *Pilgrim's Progress*. Maybe you remember the former owner...an older man, lived in the apartment on West 84th Street that you burglarized at least three times that I know of. The guy you threw off the fire escape?"

That earned me a direct look. "Who the hell are you?" he said. "And what are you talking about? I work in a bookstore, and yes, I have an interest in a rare copy of *Pilgrim's Progress*, but I don't do burglary, and I definitely don't throw people off fire escapes."

"Your colleague tells me you do, and he is willing to help me prove it to the police, for a price."

"Uh-huh. And you're here looking after my interests, right?"

"No, actually. I'm here to see if I can make a better deal with you. I want to know who killed the old man."

"What old man?"

"Fine," I said. "Play it that way. I've got the book, and I've got Kale willing to turn you over. Have a nice day."

"Wait. Wait a minute," he said. He checked his reflection in the glass window, pulled his eyebrow, dug some wax out of his ear and unfastened a button on his shirt. "What's your deal with Kale?"

"I give him the book and he gives me a hundred grand and a written statement saying it was you that killed Mr. Rupert."

"A written statement," he laughed. "Very flimsy. Wouldn't get an indictment."

"Maybe not, but it will get the cops looking hard in your direction. I wonder what they'll find."

He thought for a moment and nodded. "They get me, they get Kale, too."

"If he's still in the neighborhood. It will be a matter of timing," I said.

He nodded again. "Where's he going to get a hundred grand?"

"He told me he had a buyer lined up, not that it matters to me. The money is a bonus, as long as I get the killer. Why did you kill Mr. Rupert?"

"What kind of a deal do I get?"

"Who killed the old man?"

"Not me." He tugged at his belt, scraped the ground with his shoe and dug at a fingernail. I figured he was either flashing the bunt sign or the suicide squeeze. "The idea was to scare the old bastard into telling us where the book was," he said.

"Us? So, Kale was there, too? He killed Rupert?"

He shrugged his shoulders. "What do I get?"

"Same deal. The book, and time to read it in peace."

He looked at me again, studying me. All of his movements stopped. He moved close and just stared at me for a long, scary moment. He wasn't a big man, a little shorter than me, but with a muscular body that seemed coiled with energy.

"I'll consult with some of my advisors. How do I get in touch with you?" he said with a smile.

"You could place another ad in *American Bookman*," I said.

He glanced at the police station again, and then walked quickly away. Half a block away, he turned to smile at me again, and then turned the corner. I ran across the street to hail a cab, clutching my tape recorder. I took the cab up to Fourteenth Street, then a bus across town, and then another train uptown to the police station. Everyone around me looked like Edmund, but none of them was.

Chasko was in his cubicle, saying 'uh-huh' into his phone and staring at a computer monitor. He didn't acknowledge me when I sat in the chair next to his desk and turned on my tape recorder. He sighed deeply as he hung up, and stared at me dolefully as I told him about Kale and Edmund.

"You're McCullough, right? You don't have any evidence here, Mr. McCullough," he said when the short tape was finished. "You have a very imaginative story, and two barely intelligible recordings with a lot of street noise in which no one admits to anything."

"Will you at least investigate if I get one of them to accuse the other?"

He held up a thick blue binder of computer printouts. "These are manpower reports, Mr. McCullough. Do you realize what an investigating detective costs for an eight-hour day, between salary and benefits? My captain, and therefore this precinct, is dedicated to containing the cost of police work under his command. That means no frivolous investigations."

"Frivolous," I said. "One death, one nervous collapse, three break-ins, and a historical artifact worth at least a hundred thousand dollars doesn't seem frivolous."

"It's a matter of perspective, Mr. McCullough, like a lot of things in life. A suicide, a questionable burglary where nothing was stolen, and a fairy tale are, in police terms, frivolous."

"Will you at least do a background check on them? Maybe one of them has a record or something."

"No," he said. "Not for the likes of you." The phone rang, he turned away from me to answer it, and our interview was over.

On the way out, I said to the empty stairway, "The likes of me?"

~ * ~

I took a train back to The Battery, and then a bus up Broadway to Spring. Edmund would have needed a helicopter to follow me. I was angry and frustrated, although not surprised by Chasko's attitude, and at least I still had the book.

At home later that afternoon, after another marathon vacuuming session, I called Paulie. "Are you settled in?" I asked. "You may need to be there for a few more days."

"I think that may not be a problem, Arthur," he said. "Peggy seems to like having me around. Some kind of a mother instinct, I guess. I do get the feeling something's wrong, though."

"What do you mean," I asked.

"Well, she seems so sad sometimes. And angry, too. I think something is going wrong in her marriage. I asked about her husband and she almost ran out of the room. Something is troubling her, I'm sure of it. I think she may be afraid of her husband. I haven't even seen him yet."

"He hasn't come home?" I asked.

"Not a sign of him."

"What do you know about the guy? About her marriage? I met a cop out there the other day, and got a strange look when I mentioned the name Emerson."

"I know she's been married to him for only about ten years, and was pretty much on her own for a long time before that. He seems to be a well-respected business man in this neighborhood. She has plaques hanging in the den." The term 'highly respected business man' can carry several shades of meaning. Ivan Boesky was a highly respected business man at one point. "I have been wondering if maybe I should just go home."

"I don't think home is a good idea yet, Paulie. But if you're concerned, why don't you call Eugenia?"

"I did call her. Marguerite's idea, really. But, well, you know Eugenia, the queen of drama. She thinks it would be inappropriate for me to stay there because we're not married. People would talk. Can you imagine?"

"Having met Mrs. Federico, yes, I can imagine. But on a different tack, Paulie, what do you know about Walter's ancestors?"

"Oh, just a little. He talked a lot about them, but he mostly told the same stories over and over. Why?"

"Well, I thought it might help if I had an idea where the book came from. Did he ever happen to mention when it came into his family?"

"Well, I know his people came over from Germany. Hanover or maybe Hamburg, I think, in the early eighteen hundreds. There was a flood of immigration from Europe at the time, out of fear and religious repression and, who was that guy, oh, Napoleon. It can be such a sad world, Arthur. It's a wonder it doesn't collapse from sorrow."

"Yeah, yeah, I—

"I used to perform an old Indian folk tale with exactly that title, *The World Collapses in Sorrows*. It was about the horror of the Trail of Tears..."

"Well, yeah, I'm sure, but what about the book?"

"Oh, they didn't have the book then. The book was from the time of the Civil War. I'm pretty sure."

"Did any of Walter's people serve in the Civil War?"

"I can't remember him ever saying one way or the other, but I could ask Peggy. She may know." Peggy again. McGill, called Lil, known as Nancy.

"Tell me, what is it with her name? Is she Marguerite, or is she Peggy?"

"Peggy was just, I guess, a nickname she grew out of. By the time she was in high school, she was Marguerite, especially when Walter was yelling at her. Why?"

"Well, I don't want to ruin your faith, Paulie, but do you remember Walter's journal? He said there was a phone call and an argument with 'P'. I am wondering if that was Peggy."

A long silence. I imagine there was a sequence of facial expressions from disbelief to anger.

"No," he said finally. "Walter would have said something to me. Peg...Marguerite would have mentioned she'd been in touch with her father. No. You're on the wrong track. Totally the wrong one."

"Well, don't mention any of this to her. It probably isn't that important, and she seems to have enough to deal with right now."

"And she thinks the whole thing about the book is silly anyway. A wild goose chase. I have to admit," he sighed, "if it weren't for Walter's death, I would start to wonder myself."

"Don't lose faith, Paulie," I said. "I'm sure something is going to turn up soon. I'm very sure."

"Do you have any leads yet, Arthur? Any new information?"

"Well, I think I'm making some progress, but I don't have anything definite yet. I did visit the bookstore that made the five hundred dollar offer." I decided not to tell him I had found the book, or about my discussions with Messrs. Kale and whoever. Or the conversation with Bernard. I didn't want Peggy/Marguerite to know. She, and her missing husband, were turning into another thread to pull on.

"Well, that's something, I suppose. What do you plan to do next?"

Good question. "I'm going to wait a few days and if nothing develops, I'm going to visit Kale and Edmund again at the Grove Street Bookstore."

"What did you say that name was?"

"Kale, like that god-awful purple cabbage. He's the owner of the bookstore."

"No, the other name. Edward?"

"No, Edmund. Why do you ask?"

"Oh, no reason. Just curiosity."

Nine

I swept and scrubbed my apartment the next day, and again the day after that. I was careful with the sambuca, but found myself hearing westbound airplanes all day long. And just for the hell of it, I looked up and called the number for Emerson & Wycoff, Architects. Mr. Emerson was not in, and was not expected today.

I called Bernard Prowse at his bookstore, but he said he didn't have any information for me yet and I'd just have to be patient for a few days. And he threw in a short lecture that started with 'You kids today.' I needed a nap, tired probably from the tension of confronting Edmund and Kale, and from being patronized by Chasko. When I woke up, it was almost dinnertime, and I had nothing in the apartment to eat. I threw on a hoodie and dragged my sluggish carcass to the market.

I picked up what I thought would last me for about three days, my personal best, and packaged it carefully for the four-block walk home. I stood in front of the elevator, holding one bag of groceries and balancing the other between my chin and my knee. Just as I was reaching for the elevator key in my pocket, something stung me on the ear lobe.

I heard Kale's voice. "It seems now you are the one at a disadvantage, Mr. McCullough." I tried to turn around and felt something hard against the back of my head.

"What you feel is an automatic pistol with enough power to shatter your skull, and impel pieces of bone and brain out through your forehead. I personally abhor violence, but as Montaigne once wrote, 'Necessity is a violent school mistress and teacheth strange lessons.' Please use your key to open the door."

I opened the elevator, and the three of us got on. Kale smiled and rocked back and forth on his heels. Edmund held the gun against my head.

The elevator stopped at the fifth floor and we stood in silence in front of the big doors for a full minute.

"What?" Edmund barked.

"You need the other key," I said. "Left side jacket pocket."

He slapped me across the side of the head and then ripped my jacket pocket getting the key out. His hands were trembling as he put the key in the lock. "Don't even try to be funny," he said as he pushed me out of the elevator.

"Edmund is nervous," Kale said, "and when nervous he's highly dangerous. I suggest you try very hard to do everything he asks, and perhaps to even anticipate his needs."

I stood in the main room holding the bags of groceries while the two of them looked around. Kale said, "A nice home, Mr. McCullough. Nicely appointed, except in those regions clearly under construction. I give you credit for more esthetic sense than common sense." Edmund walked around inspecting everything, occasionally touching something, and glaring at me.

"Where is it?" he said. I stood still, holding the bags and looking off at nothing. He strode up to me, put the gun to my nose and pulled the hammer back. The click of that hammer is the loudest noise I have ever heard. I closed my eyes and waited, almost certain I was about to be shot through the head. I wanted to tell him. I wanted to say the words 'safety deposit box' because I knew that's what the gun wanted me to do, and the gun was in complete control of my life. It wasn't the guy holding it. I couldn't even think as far as him. I wasn't even able to reason that, if I told him, he would no longer have any reason to delay shooting me. I only wanted to make the gun happy. To please it into not going off. But I couldn't move. I couldn't coordinate the words with my breath and vocal cords and mouth. I couldn't even make a poor attempt. So, I just stood there in my living room holding two bags of groceries waiting to get shot through the head.

"There is really no need for a lot of fuss," Kale said. "If the book is here, give it to us. If it is somewhere else, just tell us where it is and we'll let you go."

I still couldn't speak. The gun was pressed up against my nose so tightly it was bringing tears to my eyes. I could smell the oil and feel the slight tremble in Edmund's hand. My own arms were beginning to tremble from the weight of the packages.

"Edmund, put the gun down," Kale said. "Put it down! He's not going to tell us anything that way."

Without moving the gun, Edmund drew closer and grabbed me by the hair. "Perhaps we can think of another way."

"Of course there is another way, you idiot!" Kale snapped. Edmund's glare turned from me to Kale, but he said nothing as he lowered the gun.

"Please put the packages down on the table, Mr. McCullough. Let's have a civilized little discussion."

"Fine," Edmund said to me. "Discuss. But while you do, just keep in mind this sequence. First, you chat with the brains of the operation here. Then, things around here get broken. Then, parts of you get broken, one by one, until I have my book."

I put the groceries on the kitchen table and sat down, still watching Edmund and the gun as they moved away from me. Kale smiled and said, "Violence is not required, not *de rigueur,* as it were. Negotiation remains our optimal path. We don't want to harm you, Mister McCullough. We only want your cooperation."

My brain was slowly coming to life again. My cognitive skills seemed to increase in direct proportion to my distance from Edmund and his pistol.

"How did you find me?" I asked.

He laughed. "We didn't need to find you, Mr. McCullough, or may I be familiar and call you Arthur? We have always known where you are."

"Shut up, Kale. Stop playing host, or Master of Ceremonies, or whatever little performance is going on in your head. Just shut up. He needs to come clean with us. We don't need to tell him anything. You keep it shut or I may just shoot you." He was standing next to my phone, and I could see the small red light flashing on the answering machine. Edmund practiced his feral glare at both of us for another moment, and then went back to investigating my loft.

"Edmund has been fortifying himself for this confrontation, Arthur."

"Fortifying," I said. That was fairly easy to interpret.

"We have had you figured out since the funeral," Edmund called across the room. "And I just have to say, staying in the old man's apartment that night was really very stupid." Remembering Jonesy's face, I could only agree.

"I know you're scared of him," Kale whispered to me. "And absent your cooperation, I'll have no choice but to let him at you. I imagine he has torture in mind. Nothing really creative, I'm sure, just the standard brute violence. Blood, broken bones, swollen, pulpy flesh. Very unpleasant, and very avoidable."

"And yet still very preferable to being dead."

He smiled at me. "You and I seem to have switched roles since our last meeting. At first I didn't believe your assurances, and now you don't believe mine. Perhaps we can come to some mutually agreeable method of ensuring your safety after you give us what we want. Suppose we take you to some suitable public place and you tell us there."

"And tomorrow? What keeps me safe tomorrow? I know you two killed someone and I know why. If I give you the book, how are you going to let me live?"

He looked quickly over his shoulder. Edmund was at the far corner of the living room. The phone was on a small end table near the doorway to the music room, blinking timidly, waiting patiently to share its message.

"I never killed anyone," Kale whispered, "nor did I wish harm to the old man. I only wanted the book. I have found, like General Patton, that it is useless to tell someone how to do a job. It is sufficient to tell them what needs to be done, and they will generally surprise you with their resourcefulness. Edmund certainly did surprise me, and that was my one mistake in this whole affair. I don't think General Patton ever commanded anyone quite as volatile as Edmund."

"You were very surprised when I told you Walter Rupert was dead. And yet, you knew about the funeral. So, yeah, I don't have a very good reason to trust what you say."

He straightened up and stared at me for a moment. "All the world's a stage, Arthur. I was just playing the part written for me."

We watched Edmund climb the stairs to my bedroom area. I could see him pulling the bedclothes apart, lifting the mattress, looking under the bed. When he was satisfied the book was not there, he quickly made the bed, tucked in the corners, and rearranged the pillows.

"There is still a chance you and I can come to an agreement," Kale said, "independent of Edmund."

Kale was afraid of him too; I could see it in his face.

"I believe it was Barney Fife who first made clear for us that there is no honor among thieves."

"What happened in here?" Edmund called. "What is all this white powder?"

"Plaster dust," I called back. "I just removed the plaster from a wall, and it's still settling."

"Pretty stupid thing to do. What a mess." He was in the music room now, moving shelves and instruments, and whatever else was moveable in there. The phone and blinking answering machine were about halfway between where Kale and I sat, and where we watched for Edmund to emerge. *Maybe Paulie called*, I thought.

"What kind of an agreement?" I asked.

"Very similar to what you offered to me. Give me the book and forget about everything else. I'll give you a detailed written statement about how and why Edmund killed the old man, as well as a few other transgressions of the penal code." He showed me a pair of handcuffs in his pocket.

"You can walk away from this safely, Mr. McCullough," he said. "We only need to get him to put that gun down."

Edmund came out of the music room and walked slowly to the bookshelves near the front door. He held the gun loosely in his left hand as he walked. He crouched down to the lower shelf of books, put the gun down on the floor and started looking through them slowly. He was careful and meticulous, looking intently at each and then putting it back where it had been.

"Books," he said, when he reached the end of the bottom shelf. "I'm sick to death of books. When we finally cash this one in, I'm going somewhere where people keep warm by burning books."

"Why don't we start with a more neutral question?" Kale said loudly, for Edmund's benefit. "Where exactly did you find it?"

"I'm not sure you'll believe me," I said. Maybe Chasko had called and left a message. Or maybe it was Mr. Prowse with news.

"It's been said, by Oscar Wilde I believe…"

Edmund screamed. He ran across the room and grabbed Kale by the back of his collar. He slammed him backwards into the refrigerator, yanked him forward and slammed him back again. "No more of your stupid quotes! I won't tell you again to shut up!" Kale wiped some blood from his nose and said nothing.

"Let me tell you a few things you may not know," Edmund said to me in a high-pitched and strangled voice. "I am a rational man in an irrational society. I am only destructive when necessary and only to the degree necessary. Unlike my partner, I value people more than things, so I will begin by breaking things until you tell me what I want to know. But when I become tired of breaking things, I will start hurting people. That book belongs to me, and I am going to get it. I may need to break everything in this apartment, I may even need to break you, but I will get it." This little speech sounded as if it had been rehearsed, possibly for my benefit. I could imagine him in front of a full-length mirror, twirling his gun and practicing his lines.

"Edmund," Kale said softly. "I think there is another way. Mr. McCullough and I were just beginning to narrow our differences. This is just a matter of the right leverage. I think a few minutes more of negotiations and we can get what we need without violence."

"Fine. You professors talk. I'll keep looking. It seems to be what I do best, and what I've had the most practice at. By the way," he said to me, "where do you keep your rags?"

He got a rag from under the kitchen sink, let some water run on it and wiped the fine layer of plaster dust off the counter and kitchen table. Then he walked over to the parakeets and scraped the gun butt across the metal bars of the cage, sending them flapping and screeching.

I looked at Kale and nodded. "Okay, I'll cooperate," I whispered. "How can we get the gun?"

"Tell him it's hidden behind something heavy. He'll need to use both hands, and I can get it away from him then. As soon as I'm pointing it at him, put the cuffs on. We are counting on each other, Mr. McCullough. Please do not let me down."

"Edmund!" Kale called. But Edmund was occupied. He was wiping down my phone and noticed the flashing light. He pushed the playback button.

"Mr. McCormick, McDougal, or whatever you call yourself, this is Mrs. Shaw, yes that Mrs. Shaw. Jonesy's mother. I have not heard from my daughter yet, and I am assuming you have. I learned years ago that feckless boyfriends take priority over dedicated mothers. I realize you and I are not on the most cordial terms, but surely you can appreciate a mother's concern for her daughter. Please call me. I am staying at her apartment for a few days. Please don't come, just call."

Edmund turned to us with a wide grin. "Leverage," he said as he paged through my address book. "Leverage has come to us in the person of Mrs. Shaw, mother of Jonesy, currently in residence at 459 East 73rd Street, apartment 6-A."

"Potentially, the late Mrs. Shaw of 459 East 73rd Street," said Kale. "I believe Mr. McCullough's cooperation is now assured."

I walked into the music room with Edmund, the gun and Kale following close behind. I turned on the stereo and pushed the button to pop out the CD tray. Taped to the underside of the tray was a small brown envelope with two safety deposit box keys.

"Chemical Bank on Hudson Street," I said. "I'll have to go with you. They know me there."

~ * ~

I made dinner for them, just toast and eggs, with Edmund watching me and Kale taking a turn inspecting my loft. Edmund was calmer now, the gun tucked into the waist of his pants. He was coaching third again, making those constant small movements, and avoiding eye contact.

"Where did you find the book?" he asked. "I looked everywhere in the old bastard's room."

I didn't answer.

"Probably not a good idea to piss me off right now. Where did you find that damned book?" He spun me around and cuffed my hands behind my back.

"The old guy was too smart for you," I said.

He stuck a finger in my ear. "Not quite the illuminating answer I was hoping for. Wanna try again before I look for something else to stick in there?"

"You won't like it," I said. "He faked you out of your Nikes."

"Let's see what kind of metal things I can find in the kitchen," he said.

"Okay, okay. He hid the book in your bookstore. He tucked it in with the cookbooks."

Kale overheard us. "Oh, marvelous," he said. "Out of our Nikes, indeed. Nike, by the way, was a Greek goddess..."

"Hey!" Edmund screamed. "I'm not gonna keep warning you." Kale came down the stairs, but quietly.

"Cookbooks," Edmund mumbled.

"Yep. Cost me two ninety-five."

It took him a second to process that. "The book you bought? That was actually it? I was right about him. He really was one foxy old coot. Hid it right under our noses. How could we have been so stupid?"

"It's usually hereditary," I said. He held up his hand and threatened to backhand me.

"Don't press your luck, smart-ass. You aren't out of this yet. Tell me what else you know about the book."

"You've seen the stain, the inscription and the initials. The rest should be obvious."

"Um-hm. Obvious. What do you think it's worth?"

"I would think Kale would be a better judge of that. He's the book expert." He looked disappointed at that answer, and started walking around the kitchen again, opening drawers and moving things around.

"Can I ask you a question?"

"I don't owe you anything."

That wasn't quite a no, so I asked him, "Why did you only search Mr. Rupert's bedroom? What made you so sure it would be there?"

"I know that old man. I know him like I know myself. People like us keep important things nearby."

"How did you get in? There was nothing broken."

"The old bastard was so arrogant, he opened the window for me. I had a yellow sticky note with my name on it taped to the window. So, he knew who I was, and didn't care."

"Why did you kill him?"

He looked at me for a long moment, not with anger or malice, but with thoughtfulness. As if he had never considered the question before. "Because he deserved it," he said finally.

I nodded as if I agreed, and decided to push the envelope. "You said, 'people like us.' You two are in the same club somehow?"

"Shut up," he said. "Your next mistake is going to get you hurt."

~ * ~

They took turns watching me through the night, even though I was handcuffed to the bed. Kale sat in the big room and read a book while Edmund lay on the couch.

I lay with my back to him, making him a little less ominous. "How did you get mixed up in this," he asked me, "And what do you expect to get out of it?"

"I've known Paulie for years," I said. "I do his taxes."

"You're an accountant? I should have guessed that. You look like an accountant. You got an accountant's fat ass."

"I also have a PI license," I defended myself. "That's why he asked me to help."

"And how big a piece are you getting out of it?"

"The last number we discussed was twenty-five percent." Despite the Baltimore Catechism, lying to him was easy.

That got him sitting up. I think he had been looking for a number, any kind of number to help make the whole adventure real.

"Twenty-five percent of what? You got a ball park figure?"

That surprised me. "You mean you don't know? Everyone I talk to tells me the book is worthless, and now you don't know what it's worth? Great. I've been kidnapped, handcuffed and had a gun pointed at my nose and it's maybe all for nothing."

"Yeah, for nothing. So why don't you just give it up, and you can go on your merry way."

"That's my plan. Bank deposit box tomorrow, toss the damn thing to you, and get back to my life. Just not worth getting shot over. Probably not worth anything, anyway. Not like it's diamonds or anything. How in hell can an old book be worth, I don't know, all of this."

"I don't know. The roommate doesn't know?"

"All he knows is that he inherits it."

"The hell he does. It's not his."

"I bet your partner doesn't even know."

That was the end of that conversation. He went back to coaching third base for a while, a difficult task while sitting on a couch and scowling.

Later, while Kale snored, Edmund began to clean again, systematically wiping the plaster off everything in my apartment. I could hear him prowling around, touching things, trying everything

I owned. I heard a few brief moments from the stereo, the CD player and the TV, and a few futile toots into my saxophone. I stared at the ceiling most of the night, watching the big fan blades rotate slowly and planning what I would do tomorrow. There were no encouraging scenarios. Kale had proved he couldn't be trusted, and Edmund was altogether too unpredictable. Something might develop if I could get them arguing again, which wouldn't be much of a challenge, but I wasn't sure what it would get me. I finally fell asleep about 4 o'clock, and dreamed about batteries with pathetic little legs running down a hill.

~ * ~

"It doesn't really make sense for both of us to accompany Mr. McCullough to the bank," Kale said to Edmund over coffee the next morning. "A parade of people might look suspicious."

"So, you're suggesting I should go alone, and you'll be waiting here," Edmund said.

"Actually, I was suggesting that I go, and you wait for us somewhere nearby. I think I'm better qualified to judge whether or not it's the genuine article."

"No," said Edmund. "That won't work. I have a reason to come back. You don't."

I saw a chance to add a little fuel to the fire.

"Which one of you put the ad in the *American Bookman.* Box #277086, looking for a buyer for the *Pilgrim's Progress?*"

Edmund jumped up and grabbed me around the neck. "I told you not to press your luck. You're not out of this yet." He shook me a few times and then pushed me down into a chair.

"Edmund," said Kale. "I can't believe you don't trust me. We've been in this together from the beginning, let's not fall apart now."

"Yes, from the beginning," Edmund said slowly. "From the beginning I told you everything I know. I told you who, I told you what, and I told you where. And you still won't tell me why."

Kale shook his head and turned to me. "I think Aesop had some classical wisdom related to gratitude...something about a lion and a mouse. I don't quite see myself as a lion, however, in contrast to..."

"That's it!" Edmund yelled. He pulled the gun from his belt and pointed it at Kale's nose, exactly the way he pointed it at mine the day before. No one moved, or spoke, and there was no sound except the hum of the refrigerator. After about three deep breaths, Edmund pulled the gun back slowly.

Please, please, I thought. *Don't.*

"You stay there," he barked at Kale. "You come with me." He pushed me down on the floor, adjusted the handcuffs around a radiator, and went back to Kale.

Kale was white with fear. "Edmund, you're right. I have not treated you fairly, but that will cease as of now. Right now. Just let me make things right."

"Fine, for starters, tell me about the book. Why it's valuable and who we can sell it to."

"Oh, my dear boy. My dear, dear partner…"

"Enough," Edmund said softly, and smacked Kale, open handed, across the head. Kale went down to his knees. Edmund hit him again, and a third time. "Who is the buyer?"

"Okay, I'll tell you, just let me get up."

"Get up and I'll knock you down again. Who is the buyer?"

Kale hesitated took a deep breath, and apparently decided he had no choice but to tell the truth.

"I don't have one. Yet."

"You son of a bitch. You've been playing me from the start," Edmund said. He gave him two sharp kicks in the ribs, and then walked around and kicked him on the other side.

He pointed at me. "Rope," he said. "You have rope around this museum somewhere. Where?"

He tied up Kale like he was a steer in a rodeo; on his belly with his hands behind his back and lashed to his legs. There was another rope around his neck tied to the radiator next to me.

"Edmund," Kale said in a strangled voice, "I'm having trouble breathing. Please, at least turn me over."

Edmund smiled and kicked him in the ribs. "Tell me," he said.

"Let me up and I'll tell you."

"Backwards. Tell me and I'll let you up. Who is the buyer?" Another kick followed only by labored breathing from Kale.

He pulled the gun and said to me, "You give me any trouble and you'll get the same thing. Get up and let's go." We had to step over Kale to get out.

~ * ~

For some reason, I have a perfectly clear recollection of the next ten minutes, both sight and sound, and the memory hasn't faded at all in the months since. Edmund walked on my left, hands in his pockets, the gun pressing just slightly against my side. It was about 10:30, and the streets were fairly busy. I remember passing under a man on a fire escape playing John Cougar Mellencamp's "Small Town." My karma dictated that he was singing the last verse, about dying in a small town.

While waiting to cross Broadway, I heard a guy tell his friend, "It goes along with my theory. The smaller the backpack, the cuter the chick." A guy in a pickup truck was screaming at a cabbie who had cut him off.

Edmund would jam the gun into my side every few minutes and tweak me about Mrs. Shaw.

"Girlfriend's mom, huh? Sometimes that's a turn on. Is she young? Sounded kind of hot on the phone. Maybe we could...no, never mind. I'm going to be busy reading my book. Sounded like she didn't like you anyway. I think you give off a certain aura." He gave me a sharp poke in the ribs.

I said, "I hope you enjoy reading your book because the only person who knows how to cash it in is gasping for air in my living room."

"Don't worry about it," he said, but without the expected poke.

Chemical Bank is a small building, decorated in that typically charming bank style that suggests in a refined way, 'leave your money here and go away.' The managers and vice presidents and loan officers sit at window desks around the perimeter of the building, and not one of them looks like Clark Kent, or even Elliot Ness. There is a round counter in the center with withdrawal and deposit forms, and a half dozen pens that don't work. The safety deposit boxes are down a short corridor opposite the bank entrance and there is a small wooden desk at the entrance to the corridor where a neatly dressed and energetic Black woman sat.

Edmund grabbed my arm as we went in. "Show me the key," he said. I pulled it from the small brown envelope and held it out to him.

"Be quick and be smart," he said, and then whispered, "459 East 73rd St., Apartment 6A."

I walked to the desk. "I'd like to get my box, please," I said.

"Sure thing," she said, with a smile of recognition. "How have you been?"

"Oh, just fine, thanks." She showed me where to sign, and then compared my signature with the one in her book. As I handed her the key, I glanced over my shoulder. Edmund faced the other way, rummaging through the brochure rack. I thought of whispering to her to call the police, but couldn't think of a way to convince her without him knowing. I was afraid he wouldn't hesitate to shoot her, and turn this into a complete slaughter.

She unlocked the little door with the two keys, pulled out my box and handed it to me. I smiled at her, stepped into the small room and locked the door. I pulled the cell phone out of the flat metal box, flipped it open and punched 911. Nothing. No lights, no beeps, nothing. I shook it and tapped it and dialed again. Nothing. The battery was stone dead. So much for being prepared. I grabbed the small book in its blue velvet bag, slipped the other book in my jacket, closed the box and left. As I handed the box back to the lady, I glanced at Edmund. He was leaning against the counter, hands in his pocket and his eyes fixed on the small blue package in my hand. *Good. Focus on that.*

He grabbed it from my hand and pulled the book from the bag. "Betty Crocker," he read slowly. "You got the wrong—"

I hit him with the cell phone, aiming for his ear. The phone was too light, though, and Edmund too quick. He ducked, and the glancing blow knocked him back against the counter. I saw the dark metal of the gun come out of his pocket. I slapped at it with the remnants of the phone and knocked it out of his hand. It skidded across the tile floor and came to a stop about two feet in front of a startled security guard. Edmund bolted for the door, and I felt two arms wrap around me and pull me to the ground.

"Stop him!" I yelled. "Call the police. He kidnapped me. He's on his way to a woman's apartment on 73rd Street. Someone please call and warn her. Please call her right away."

When the police arrived, it took me almost half an hour, and all of my identification, to convince them I was a regular customer of this bank, and that Jonesy's mother was in danger. They called her apartment, but only got her answering machine. They promised to send a squad car.

After finally getting someone to half-believe my story, I was escorted back to my apartment with two uniforms. I tried to talk to them, but they just nodded and said, 'Okay,' like I was a psycho-phone-breaker-serial-bank brawler that had to be treated gently. Kale was where we had left him, still breathing, and a few minutes later an ambulance came to take him away. He wasn't dead, but looked to be close to it.

For the next few hours, people streamed in and out of the loft. Detectives, uniformed cops, photographers, assistant cops and assistant photographers. They moved around my loft like the walking dead, murmuring to each other and working hard to look like what they were doing was important. No one introduced themselves, and most of them paid no attention to me. I told my story to a man in a blue suit, then to a woman in a brown suit, and then answered a lot of questions from a trio of people, one of whom had a sketchpad. After they left me alone, I sat by the phone hitting the redial button every five minutes and swearing at the beginning of Jonesy's message. "I'm either out shopping or taking pictures somewhere. If it's pictures, I'll be home soon to return your call. If I'm shopping, well, who knows?"

I was listening to that for about the ninth time when Chasko walked in, looking very mortal. When it all spooled out, this episode probably wouldn't be a feather in his cap. I couldn't tell if he was trying to look sincerely official or officially sincere.

He tried a smile, but I didn't react, so he just nodded. "We have a positive ID on the man who was injured here," he said.

"Sure," I said. "Lloyd Kale. He's one of the men I told you about yesterday."

"Yes," he said, looking down at his notebook. "He owns a bookstore on—"

"Grove Street," I interrupted. "The Grove Street Bookstore. Established 1931. That's where I found Mr. Rupert's worthless book. The one they came here to get. Kale runs the bookstore with the guy who smacked him around and tied him up. The guy whose fingerprints are all over this loft, and all over the gun from the bank."

"Yes," he said again. "We're trying to match those prints. What else can you tell me about—"

"Edmund. Not much. I never even got his last name. I've already described him and your artists have generated a good sketch of him." He nodded.

"You'll be happy to learn the woman you were concerned about is safe. She was intercepted outside the residence and is now at her daughter's apartment. And by the way, the daughter is there, too."

"The daughter is there, too? The daughter?"

"Yes. While the patrolmen were waiting with the mother, she just walked in with her suitcase. Says she just got off a plane from, I think Montana."

"Wisconsin."

"Right, Wisconsin. We'll keep a uniformed guard posted."

"That's just amazing. Hard to believe, but the best news I've heard all day. And you're gonna keep a guard there, right?"

"Yes, it's already on the books for twenty-four hours."

"Oh, all those man-hours."

"I'm tired, Mr. McCullough," he sighed, "and I don't need your sarcasm."

"Sarcasm," I said. "What you called a suicide was a murder. The burglaries you said didn't happen, really did happen. The tape you said was worthless will probably be prime evidence at a murder trial.

One of the men you said was probably harmless almost killed the other one after they broke into my home at gunpoint. Sarcasm. Right."

He stood up to leave, but then changed his mind. "I know about you," he said, angry now, pointing his finger at me. "I checked into your PI license and found out some interesting things, Mr. McCullough. I know all about you and I know about your father. Your father was a crook, and you are, too. He's been ripping the little guy off for decades, and you live in a building purchased with some of that stolen money. You're as corrupt as he is, so don't you dare be sanctimonious with me." He glared at me for another moment and then walked out. I stared at the door for a few minutes, thinking of something to say. Trying, again, to come up with some kind of defense, something that would make it not true. But the door didn't melt, Chasko didn't burst into flames, and when I finally looked away, it was all still true.

Within half an hour, the rest of them had filtered out as well, with their guns and notepads and preconceived notions still intact.

I called Jonesy at her mother's. I couldn't do small talk just then, so I just said, "Hi, it's me."

"Are you all right?" she asked. "What happened? Where are you?"

"I'm home. I'm fine. Listen, cops will be there until tomorrow, but then I want you and your mother to leave. Go get a motel room somewhere for a couple of days. Go to Europe. Go to the Bahamas."

"Why? What's going on? The cops wouldn't tell me anything."

I took a deep breath. "The guys that killed Mr. Rupert came here looking for his book. They heard your mom's phone message, and found your address. They threatened to come after her if I didn't give it to them." I told her briefly about Kale and how I got away from Edmund. "I'm safe now, I think, but he's still out there. I just want to be sure you're safe, too."

"Who are these people? How did they find you?" There was just a hint of panic in her voice, which, for my sins, made me feel a little better.

"I don't know how, but they did. The point is one of them is still out there. Please, Jonesy, just do it. Just go and stay somewhere else for a couple of nights."

"Okay," she said at last. "I will. We will."

When I hung up, I was finally, finally alone, but there was something wrong, something different about the loft. I looked over at the spot where Kale had lain, and remembered the soft thud of the kicks, and the raspy breath. The smell of the bacon and pancakes I had made for breakfast still hung in the air. There was a smell from the cops, too: cigarettes, coffee and large bodies in the middle of a long day. But none of that bothered me. There was something different about my home, about the loft itself. I realized it wasn't secure anymore. I'd been hiding up there for years, swaying with the breezes, watching from a safe distance as the earthbound ones scrambled and scrapped and got screwed. But after today, my sanctuary wouldn't be safe anymore. My tree house had been climbed.

I closed all the blinds and drapes, checked to be sure all the doors and windows were locked, put a chair under the doorknob, and then crashed on the couch.

Ten

The phone woke me in the middle of the next afternoon from a deep sleep. A sing-songy voice I didn't quite recognize said. "Would you hold a minute please, Mister Bird?"

"He's here, Mr. McCullough," Mrs. Emerson's voice said.

"What?" I said. There was some mumbling and then Paulie came on the line. "He's here, Arthur," Paulie said.

"Paulie, what is it? Who's there?" More mumbling, and then a brief silence that let me wake up enough to realize this wasn't part of a nightmare. Although it really was.

"I have a small steak knife in the old man's ear," Edmund said. "I think if I push just hard enough, it will go through his ear drum and into his brain, but I'm not sure. It's something I've always wanted to try."

"I'll bring you the book," I said.

"If it doesn't work the first time, there's always the other ear. There's also the area at the soft part of the palate."

"I'll bring it, I swear," I said. "I have it here and I'll bring it as fast as I can."

"You told me that before, and look where we are now."

"I'll bring it this time, I swear I will. Just don't hurt anyone."

"No tricks this time. You come quick, you come alone and you bring the right goddamn book." I heard one last grunt from Paulie and the line went dead.

I hit rush hour traffic going through the Holland Tunnel, and had time to wonder how Edmund had found Paulie. How did he know so much? He knew the book was hidden in Rupert's room, he knew Paulie would be out of his apartment on the day of the funeral, he knew where I lived, and now he knew where Paulie and Mrs. Emerson were. I could not believe it was Paulie. Or that he was partners with Mrs. Emerson. Was it the husband, Phil Emerson? And where was Phil now?

Traffic finally cleared around the rotten egg smell of Elizabeth, and within a few minutes I was doing eighty, pretty much top speed for the old Skylark, and wondering why so many BMWs and Mercedes were passing me. As I pulled up to the brick Tudor on Lake Vista Lane, the sun was low enough to be in my eyes whenever one of those curved streets turned me west. The street was empty, like suburban streets always seem to be, and the house was silent. A light was on at Burkie's house, but I couldn't see a way she could help me. There were no instructions in neon outside the house. No secret entrance that I could see. No Marines, no cavalry. Just me and a small book.

I pulled into the driveway and walked slowly up the flagstone path to the front door. Just as I was reaching for the doorbell, I heard Edmund's muffled voice call out, "Hold it up to the window."

I pulled the book out of my pocket and held it up to the glass of the front door. "Open it and let me see one of the pages."

I opened it and held it up again. "Keep both hands on the book high over your head." The door opened and as I stepped through, he grabbed the book from my hand and knocked me down.

"I owe you," he said, pointing at me with a thin, wood handled steak knife. It wasn't really much of a weapon, but it was enough. "You made a fool of me," he said, "and I won't forget it."

"Where's Paulie?" I asked.

"He's fine. No puncture wounds yet. He's in the other room with her."

"How did you get here?" I asked. "How did you know Paulie was here? How long have you been following me?"

He laughed. "Following you? You sap. We haven't been following you, we've been leading you. You're some detective."

Mrs. Emerson came out of Paulie's bedroom and looked fearfully, and hatefully, at Edmund. "Paulie?" I asked.

"He's lying down. All this has been too much for him."

"Go get me some rope," Edmund said to her. "There's some in that drawer in the kitchen. Do it quick."

He smiled at me. "We need to talk, you and I."

"You've got the book, what else do you want with me?"

"I want to know how you found it."

"He left me some hints," I said. Mrs. Emerson came into the room with the rope and Edmund tied my hands behind me.

"Don't you want to know how Kale is?" I asked.

"Not all that much. He's no good to me now."

"He's no good to anyone now. I think he may be in a coma," I said. Mrs. Emerson covered her face and turned away. I said, "He was serious about having trouble breathing. He was sort of blue when they took him away, but they think he'll live."

"Oh," he said with a little smile. "Well, I think I'll live, too, and probably much better than him. One or two more little details and I'll be living very well indeed, thank you."

Mrs. Emerson was weeping, turned toward a wall with her face still in her hands. He looked at her and held up the book. "Is this it?" he asked. "Is this finally it?"

She looked over at him and nodded.

"Get out here, old man," Edmund yelled.

"Edmund, please don't," Mrs. Emerson sobbed. "You have what you want. Please just take the book and go."

"You'll be rid of me again soon enough. Get out here right now, old man!" he yelled. "I have business to finish up."

Paulie came shuffling from the direction of the bedroom, his face red, his eyes wide. "Arthur," he said.

Mrs. Emerson turned to him, her face in terror. "Paul, I'm so sorry," she sobbed.

Edmund moved behind Paulie and put his arm around his neck. "I don't even need the knife. I can break his wind pipe and he'll choke to death right here on the floor," he said to me. "Wouldn't that be something to watch?"

"What do you want?" I asked. "You have the book. What else can I do?"

"Tell me about the book," he said. "Tell me how you found it."

"He must have known someone was after it," I said. "I told you that he switched it. He took a cookbook from a shelf in your store and replaced it with *Pilgrim's Progress*. He left a note in a diary that said 'purloined,' like in *The Purloined Letter*.

"*Purloined Letter*? What the hell is that?"

"It's just a famous detective story about how to hide things. That's how I figured it out."

"I never should have told him who I was," Edmund said.

"You saw him?" Mrs. Emerson said, almost in a whisper. "When?"

"He came into the store one day, the decrepit old bastard, trying to sell the book. I didn't recognize him until he said his name. Kale and I were trying to figure a way to get the damn book, and he just walks in with it."

"It was you, wasn't it? You killed him," Mrs. Emerson said.

"He wouldn't sell. Kale actually offered him five hundred for it, and he *still* wouldn't sell. When I said my name was Edmund, it surprised him a little, but he said he didn't care who the hell I was. I wanted to take it right then and there, but Kale thought there was an easier way. The old man came back later the same afternoon to see if we raised our offer. I guess that's when he made the switch."

"You told me Mr. Kale killed him," Mrs. Emerson said.

"Sure, I told you that. I told you a three hundred-fifty-pound asthmatic hypochondriac climbed up five stories on a fire escape and killed your father. And you believed me. You must really want to be rid of me."

"It really was you?"

He looked right at her. "Yes. It was me. He wouldn't sell it, he wouldn't give it to me and he wouldn't tell me where it was hidden. After I dragged him out of bed, I told him I was his grandson and the book was rightfully mine. That's when he slapped me. So I threw him off the fire escape. And as I was doing it, I actually thought for once in my life you might be proud of something I did. Wrong again, huh, Mom?"

"Oh, my god, Edmund."

"Yes, oh, your god. Where was God when we were living in that filthy little two room apartment? When we were eating pasta and iced tea three times a week because it was the best we could afford. Where was he?"

"I did the best I could."

"And where was Walter Lord High Almighty Rupert when I was wearing rags and having bread for lunch? For years. You told me the stories about the book. You told me stories about your mother. *You* taught me to hate that selfish grasping old bastard. *You!*"

She crumbled to her knees in tears.

He turned back to me, dragging Paulie with him like a rag doll. "Now tell me why it's so valuable. I know you shopped it around."

Paulie was standing on his toes, hanging on to the forearm against his throat, coughing and gagging. Mrs. Emerson moved slowly toward him. "You've done all this..." she said to Edmund. "You've killed your grandfather, put another man in the hospital and you don't even know why." He grabbed her by the arm and pushed her away. She fell, knocking over a shelf of potted plants and ceramic figurines.

"He was your grandfather," I said, stunned.

"Kale was the only one who knew about the book," he said, "and he wouldn't tell me. But now you know too, don't you?"

"Yes. Yes," I said, watching Paulie's face get redder. "I know something about it. It's a Civil War relic. There's an inscription on the inside to..."

With a violent scream, Mrs. Emerson came running toward Edmund with a potted plant in her hand and smashed it against the side of his head. He and Paulie went sprawling, and she picked herself up quickly and grabbed another plant pot. Edmund rolled away and I saw him wipe blood away from his eyes with the hand holding the knife. Terra cotta pots are heavy, and she had hit him hard enough to shatter it. The next planter exploded against the back of his neck and he stumbled forward, dropping the knife. Paulie was yelling, "Oh! Oh! Oh!" and Mrs. Emerson was making wild, almost inhuman sounds. Edmund was on his knees, feeling around for the knife and yelling, "Goddamn it!"

I threw myself on top of the knife. He tried to push me off it, but I spun around and kicked him in the head, just as another potted plant slammed into his shoulder. He pulled himself to his feet and staggered up the stairs. The stairway had a sharp turn to the left and ended at a hallway leading to the second floor bedrooms. Mrs. Emerson grabbed a ceramic statue and smashed it, leaving a sharp, jagged edge and charged, just a few steps behind him. I glanced over at Paulie. He was pulling himself up into a crouch, dazed but apparently unhurt. Edmund was at the top of the stairway, just in front of a window, wobbling and trying to keep the blood from flowing into his eyes. Mrs. Emerson had the jagged ceramic piece in one hand and a planter in the other. She was five or six feet away, crouched and ready to unleash another bomb. I was still pulling myself to my feet and had to strain to hear what she was saying, "You did this," she whispered to him. "You've always done this. You ruined my life, you ruined my marriage, and now you've killed your own grandfather. My father! I can't cover up for you anymore. I can't. I can't. I can't. I won't!" She threw the planter and it caught him square on the hip. He spun around and the next one she threw hit him on the side of the head. He staggered back, caught the back of his leg on the sill, and tumbled through the window.

I ran past Mrs. Emerson, still crouched and breathing hard, and looked out the window. Edmund was on the ground, rolling and screaming in pain, holding his left leg. I must have had Lincoln on the brain, because the first thing I thought of, watching Edmund fall to the ground, was, *Sic semper tyrannis.*

~ * ~

The next few hours were even more confusing than the time after they carried Kale out of my apartment. Mrs. Emerson collapsed on the floor near the window, and just moaned and rolled from side to side as Paulie untied my hands. After I dialed 911, I didn't know what to report. It wasn't exactly a robbery, not exactly a break-in, and I didn't think 'assault with a potted plant' would stir up much action.

"We need cops and an ambulance," I said. "We had a burglar, and someone's been seriously hurt."

We had local cops first, then Jersey state troopers, and then an hour later, some New York City detectives who got the word that it might be Edmund. None of them, fortunately, was Chasko. Throughout all the arrivals and departures, I could hear Edmund screaming obscenities out on the side lawn. One of the troopers told me he had a compound fracture of his tibia, a deep laceration over one eye, and probably a concussion. Somehow that just didn't seem enough to me. I was hoping for some internal bleeding, some poison ivy, hemorrhoids, shingles, and perhaps a mild case of catatonia. Every scream made me feel just a little better. Finally, an ambulance arrived, wrapped him up and took him away. I didn't take the time to wave goodbye.

Mrs. Emerson sat up soon after the first platoon of police arrived, but immediately began screaming unintelligibly at her son and clawing at the men trying to hold her. There were no words to her fury, only screams. I don't think I'd ever seen such rage, and I'd never seen anyone expend so much energy over such a long time. She kept at it long after her son had been taken away, and finally was sedated and taken to a local hospital, I guess for psychiatric observation.

After they were through with Edmund and Mrs. Emerson, the medics checked Paulie over and pronounced him fit enough to travel. He had been bruised and badly frightened, and had a sore throat, but was otherwise unharmed. While the cops were dealing with the Emerson family, Paulie and I found a corner of a couch and sat, stunned and beyond thought.

Through the crowd, I saw Burkie poke her head through the door and tiptoe over to us. She was trembling with tension and fear. She held Paulie's hand, stroking it gently, and said nothing for a few minutes.

"I hate to add to all this," she said finally, "but I have a really bad feeling about Phil. I've seen lights in the garage going off and on. Sometimes the door is open, sometimes the car is gone. I am worried about him. Will you come out to the garage with me?"

I found one of the state troopers that seemed to be looking for something to do. A big guy, too, to make me feel more secure.

I got one of the medics to sit with Paulie for a minute and Burkie, the Hulk and I edged our way out the back door.

As soon as we opened the garage door, the smell hit us, and it wasn't hard to trace it to the trunk of the grey Cadillac. The trooper had a tool to open the car door, and when he popped the trunk, all three of us gagged.

A body, presumably Phil, was wrapped up in a tarp, bent at the hip to fit in the trunk.

Burkie burst into tears, and all she could say was, 'Edmund,' over and over.

~ * ~

I gave my statement to one state trooper, two detectives, a reporter, and someone who I later found out was a neighbor. They all asked the same questions, and didn't seem to understand the answers. I guess I didn't either. Finally, someone in a suit and tie, I guess he was in charge but I never got his name, told us we could go. I was almost to the door when I remembered the book. It was lying among the broken clay pots and potting soil, open to the passage where Mr. Worldly Wiseman was giving Christian wrong directions. I took it over to the cop in charge.

"This isn't important, is it?" I asked. "It belongs to Mr. Dwyer over there. It has a sentimental value, and we'd like to take it with us."

He put his glasses on and looked carefully at it. "Technically everything is evidence," he said, "but I think we have enough on this guy without charging him with stealing a book. Why do you think he wanted it so bad, anyway?"

"I'm not sure," I said honestly. "I don't think he knew exactly why he wanted it."

He handed the book back to me. "Seems pretty nutty to me," he said. "I don't remember it was ever even made into a movie."

The ride home was dark, quiet and sad. Paulie sat crouched against the door looking out the side window, clearly not in a mood to talk. I wanted to tell him what I knew about the book, mostly because I was proud of the fact that I had found out, and I wanted to tell him he was possibly a rich man. "Walter," I heard him whisper to the window. "Oh, Walter."

From the Jersey Turnpike, I watched a jet take off at Newark Airport, wished I were on it, and then thought of Jonesy. Why was she home? I turned on the classical music station and Paulie reached over without a word and turned it off. Cars pulled up beside us with dim, distant, shadow people inside them, and then moved away. We rode back to my loft in silence and in the dark, surrounded by thousands of others traveling in the same silence and darkness, with no way to reach them.

We both slept late the next morning, Paulie on my convertible couch, and I made poached eggs and Virgin Marys for brunch.

"There are some things I need to tell you about Mr. Rupert's book," I said. "Your book, actually."

"I'm not sure I want to know," Paulie said. "I already know so many things I wish I didn't know."

"This is good news, I think. It may be Walter was right all along about the book." I told him how Walter's clever clues allowed me to find it at the Grove St. Bookstore, and how Mr. Prowse had discovered the inscription on the inside cover.

"Lincoln?" he asked. "President Abraham Lincoln? You think Walter's book may have belonged to Abraham Lincoln? Then how in the world did Walter ever get it?"

"It'll take a different kind of detective to figure that out. Mr. Prowse says he knows of a historian in Massachusetts somewhere that may be able to help."

"We won't have to go to Massachusetts, will we? I think I'd like to go home and stay there. It feels like a very long time since I was home."

"We have the book, Paulie. I'm sure he'd be willing to come to us."

"If it's true about Lincoln, then it would be worth some money, wouldn't it?"

"Mr. Prowse says if it's true, it'll be worth a lot of money."

"Then all of this has been for nothing."

"I don't follow. How do you figure it was for nothing?"

"If Walter had only known it was valuable, he could have sold it years ago and lived better. Maybe treated his wife and daughter better, too. None of this had to happen."

"But Walter didn't know it," I said. "He lived his life according to what he knew and according to what he had. People make decisions with the information they have on hand. This was not Walter's fault. Walter didn't kill his wife, someone else did that. Walter didn't make Edmund a greedy psychotic. He didn't make him a thief and a murderer. You were right about Walter. He wasn't a saint, but he was a good man. That's what I'm taking away from all of this. And he was a right all along about the book. It is valuable. Maybe very valuable."

Paulie shook his head slowly. "Edmund," he said. "I didn't figure it out until just before you got there. That crazy man really was Peggy's son. Walter's grandson. When we were in there with that crazy, angry man, Marguerite told me things. Sad, tragic things about her life after she left home. Marguerite was pregnant when she left home. That was one of the reasons she and Walter were so mad at each other, and couldn't talk to each other. Walter felt she let him down and she felt like he had let her down. After she left, Walter refused to talk about her, for years, maybe decades, and I completely lost track. That's my failure in this tragedy. In all those years after Hanna died, I can remember him mentioning his daughter one time, something about Peggy and her bastard, Edmund. I guess I just forgot about him. Or maybe I just assumed he was put up for adoption. I don't know what I thought, or if I was too stupid to think at all."

"That's why they knew so much," I said. "That's how they knew where I lived. Mrs. Emerson was telling Edmund everything he needed to know."

"Don't blame her too much, Arthur. I think she's had a hard life."

"If she lived with him, she's had a hard life."

"I think maybe that's why she wanted him to have the book. I think she just wanted him out of her life. It's all horrible. Just horrible."

"There's still a lot about all of this I'd like to ask her. Do you think she would talk to me?"

He shook his head. "I don't know. She was so wild last night. I wonder if she's okay, and if she's talking to anybody."

We spent the next couple of days at my loft, just living quietly, like Travis McGee and Meyer on his houseboat after one of their exhausting adventures. Just no girls in bikinis hanging around. We slept late, ate a lot of takeout food, and watched a lot of TV. Paulie didn't talk much, and I didn't either. He mentioned going home once or twice, but not with any real enthusiasm, so I didn't press the point. Jonesy called once, just to let me know she was okay, but I let the machine answer. I knew she was safe, so I let her worry about me for a change.

On our fourth day of doing nothing, Mrs. Emerson called. Paulie answered, and I put the call on speakerphone. They had let her out of the hospital the day before with some strong tranquilizers and business cards from several good psychiatrists. The police had been to see her, but couldn't quite see that she was a suspect in any crime. She sounded weary and beaten, and she asked if she could see Paulie and me. I was about to volunteer to drive out to her house when Paulie told her to meet us at his apartment. "It's time for me to go home anyway," he said.

Next day we packed his clothes, his *TV Guide* and his medicine, and I drove him back up to 84th Street. I gave him his new set of keys and let him off in front of his building so I could find a parking spot. Walking back, I realized I should have stayed with him. It could have been a shock for him to come back to the empty apartment where so much had happened. Even the stairs alone might kill him. I ran half of the six blocks back to his building, and took the stairs two at a time.

I had flashbacks of the last time I had run up these stairs, when they were just about to carry him out, but this time I found him humming and draping a tablecloth over the kitchen table.

"I called Mrs. Lewis from your apartment the other day," he said. "She owed me a favor from a few times I did magic tricks for her little boy. She's a Black woman, or African-American, I guess, but she makes the best sauerbraten of anyone I know. Almost as good as Hanna's. Would you reach those candleholders for me up on that shelf? And you're going to need to go around to the store for me, too. Let me make a list."

When Mrs. Emerson arrived four hours later, looking drained and guilty, there was a full meal of sauerbraten and kartoffelkloess, red cabbage, wine, ice cream, and apple pie on the table. Paulie, clean pants and a shirt and tie, beamed at the doorway like a *maître d'* at a grand opening.

She sat across the table from me, avoiding eye contact. I watched her carefully, and she seemed to be doing everything more slowly and deliberately. The right drugs will do that for you. "I wasn't really expecting a meal," she said. "I really just wanted to explain. And apologize. For everything. I've been...I've been so..."

"I thought an old-fashioned German meal might help a little," Paulie said. "Like the old days."

"I remember meals like this," Mrs. Emerson said, trying to smile. "But it seems like another lifetime."

"You and your mom and dad used to have me over to dinner on Sundays and your mom would cook sauerbraten and these delicious dumplings," Paulie said.

"I guess we did have some good days in this apartment. I used to do my homework at this table. Dad always helped me with the math. Mom could never do math." She looked down at her plate for a moment and then dissolved into tears. She left the table quickly and ran to the bathroom.

"What are you working on here?" I asked Paulie.

"I'm not sure. I thought since she had no one left, and I have no one left...well, I just don't know."

She returned in a few minutes and we all sat eating quietly for a while. "This is a wonderful meal," she said finally, "but I really came here to talk to both of you. To apologize, and to try to explain what happened." She looked at Paulie. "It was really so kind of you to go to all this trouble to make me feel comfortable, and yes, in a surprising way it is good to be home. Listen to me, I said 'home'."

"Tell us, Peggy," Paulie said. "Tell us what happened."

"Edmund is what happened," she said. "I don't know if I could have continued to live with my father after my mother was killed, but the pregnancy made it absolutely impossible. The father was a boy I had a crush on in high school, and after I left home, he disappeared. I think he went into the service, but anyway I never heard from him again. I never even told him I was pregnant. I was lucky enough to get a job at a garden center on Staten Island, and managed to eke out a living for me and Edmund." She got that look again, somewhere between nostalgia and anguish. "A meager existence. I loved that job, but until Phil found me, it was just Edmund and me. And we were very poor, a single mother on minimum wage."

"Edmund," Paulie said. "I heard that name only once, I think."

She smiled at him. "I named him after a poem you used to recite for me, don't you remember? *Sir Edmund Spens*?"

"Oh, Peggy, that was so long ago, but I do remember you loved that old ballad."

She looked away, recollecting a moment from her girlhood, and Paulie looked at me with an expression I could not interpret... wistfulness perhaps, or melancholy.

"I worked at Green Aspiration for about fifteen years," she said, "and eventually became manager, and when they went out of business, I managed a down payment on a small nursery of my own in New Jersey. Not long after, I met Phil, and life got a little easier. But through it all, there was Edmund."

She sighed deeply. "From the first, he was a difficult child, and somehow he never grew out of it. He had trouble with everything in school: reading, arithmetic, and especially making friends. He could be mean, so mean." She held up her right hand and showed us that the pinky and ring finger would not quite straighten out. "He did this to me with the car door. He said it was an accident, but I know it wasn't. He was only nine years old at the time. I put him in special schools, took him to psychologists, nothing worked. His stepfather tried so hard to be patient with him, but the harder he tried, the more Edmund resented him. They had horrific fights. It caused a lot of trouble in my marriage. Before he was out of high school, Edmund was in trouble with the police. He was into drugs, burglary, I don't know what all else, and they finally caught up to him. He lived in California for a few years, doing God knows what, and then he was arrested. The two and a half years Edmund spent in prison were just about the happiest of my adult life. It was the one time I didn't have to worry about him. He met the other man, Mr. Kale, in prison. I don't know what Mr. Kale was there for, but when he mentioned he was an antique book dealer, Edmund told him all of my stories about Papa's book."

Papa, I thought. *She finally called him that.*

"When he got out of prison, he just started asking a lot of questions about my father and about the *Pilgrim's Progress*. Where did he keep it? What made it so valuable? I knew he was up to something, but I didn't know what. I knew the book was worthless, but if getting it would keep him out of my life, even for a little while, I would be glad to help."

"Did you know he planned to rob us?" Paulie asked quietly.

"No. Yes. I don't know. I didn't think about it. So much was going on at the same time. So much was going wrong. When he got out of prison, he didn't even let us know. He just showed up at home. We had changed all the locks, so Edmund just broke in, took up residence in the upper floor of the garage. Phil, that's my husband, was furious. He had a big fight with Edmund and then he had a big fight with me. I haven't seen him since. Our marriage was falling apart anyway, and Edmund coming home just collapsed it completely."

"When was this?" I asked.

"It was around the middle of July. Just a few weeks before my father was killed."

She began crying again, and we couldn't think of any way, or any reason, to stop her. When she was able to, she pulled herself together, apologized again, and left. Paulie and I, being men of different generations but of the same era, cleared the table and did the dishes.

"Does she even know about what happened to Phil?" I asked.

"Hmmm?" he said. "I'm sorry, I was thinking about that poem. The one she loved as a child. The name wasn't Edmund. It was actually Patrick. *Sir Patrick Spens*. She gave him the wrong name."

Eleven

Two weeks later, I got the call we'd been waiting for. Bernard Prowse had arranged for a William Julian of the American Antiquarian Society to meet us and take a look at the *Pilgrim's Progress*. We met them at the Sage Bookstore the next afternoon, and Mr. Julian turned out to be a youngish, plump, yuppie type, an academic who could have passed for a Wall Street lawyer. He was very brisk and serious, and seemed to know what he was talking about. He examined the book carefully, especially the dedication and signature at the front, and put one or two of the stained pages under a microscope.

When he was finished, he rubbed his eyes and chewed on the end of his glasses. "I think it might be possible," he said to Bernard.

Prowse blew out a deep breath and said, "Wow."

He turned to me. "There is a very good possibility that your book—"

"Not my book." I pointed to Paulie. "His book."

"There have been rumors about the existence of this book ever since the assassination," he said to Paulie. "Until recently, historians gave it no credence because of Whitman's tendency to embellish the truth, as only a poet can, and because of the general level of hysteria surrounding Lincoln's death. However, two recent biographers…"

"Whitman?" Paulie asked. "Who's Whitman?"

"Walt Whitman. The poet. I'm almost certain he's the W.W. that wrote the inscription. He served as a volunteer, helping the wounded near Washington D.C. at the end of the Civil War, and was a great admirer of Lincoln. These biographers have found verifiable references to a gift Whitman purportedly gave to Lincoln. Hand delivered in fact. And they've also found some evidence, a sales receipt, that Whitman purchased a copy of *Pilgrim's Progress* just prior to coming to Washington."

"So, you think," Paulie said, "Walt Whitman gave Walter's book to President Lincoln? I agree with you, Bernard. Wow."

Mr. Julian shrugged. "As I said, a lot of these kinds of stories circulated at the time of the assassination, but the book could never be found. Most people didn't believe any of it, including me, until now. But there's even more to the story. Lincoln supposedly had the book with him at Ford's theater, but it just disappeared after he was killed. Do you see this red stain?"

"Yes. Is it important?" Paulie asked.

"That's the real 'wow.' I'm certain it's blood."

There was a long pause. I think even Mr. Julian was surprised by what we were all thinking. "Lincoln's blood," said Bernard Prowse, reverently. "From his assassination at Ford's Theatre."

Paulie asked, "Is there any way of being absolutely sure this is the same book and that it's President Lincoln's blood?"

Mr. Julian nodded. "With probably about ninety to ninety-five percent certainty. The age of the book is easy, and of course Whitman's handwriting is easy to verify. The difficulty will be in proving it ever belonged to Lincoln, and that it was at Ford's Theatre with him. And as I said, this stain along the top of the pages does appear to be blood, so we can analyze it, type it and date it, and then we'll know. We have done work with a very careful and thorough forensics laboratory. They should have some answers for us in, oh, about a week."

"If it does turn out to be what you think it is, would it be worth a lot?"

"If that's really Whitman's signature, it's probably worth five or six thousand dollars. If Lincoln owned it too, it might be worth fifty or sixty thousand as a rare book."

"And if that's Lincoln's blood?"

"Then it's a national historical treasure, and the fifty grand would probably be a down payment." There was total silence in the room as Mr. Prowse looked at me, Paulie and I looked at each other, and Mr. Julian looked around at all of us.

"We do need to do some additional tests, and I would need to verify a find this big with several colleagues."

"We would rather you didn't take the book with you," I said. "Is there any other way you can test it? Take photographs or samples, or whatever else you need?"

He looked from me to Mr. Prowse and back to me again. "I can assure you it will be safe. You've seen my credentials..."

"I don't think you're aware of the recent history of this book," I said. "The last owner was thrown off a fire escape and killed. One of the book dealers who was, uh, negotiating to purchase it, is in the hospital with a severe respiratory trauma, caused by someone else trying to acquire it. This gentleman here had a knife in his ear and I had a loaded pistol pressed against my nose in order to prevent that person from acquiring it. We have become somewhat protective of it."

Mr. Prowse whistled softly and Mr. Julian actually took half a step back. "I'll send a representative from the laboratory down here as soon as I can. I suppose he can get what he needs, at least for a preliminary report, without taking the book back to the lab."

~ * ~

It was a few weeks before I saw Jonesy again. I had called her once or twice, but talking was difficult, and I couldn't quite manage to ask to see her again.

I came in from shopping, keeping it to one bag now, and she was sitting at my kitchen table with a water bottle and the Metro section of *The New York Times*. She walked slowly over and gave me one of her combination pat and hugs that I realized I was going to miss very much.

"Good?" she asked.

"Yes," I said. "Sadder and wiser, but safe. And so are you." I made a cup of tea for both of us and sat on the recliner in the main room. She sat on the couch.

"How's your mother doing?"

"No change, I'm afraid. Still my mother."

"Do you want to tell me about your trip?" I asked.

"No, because you were right and because there is so little to tell. I knew you were right the day I went to visit Paul at the hospital, but I had to go anyway. I almost didn't get on the plane, but I had to."

"How bad was it?"

"I don't think it was bad, it just wasn't anything. Everybody was very friendly, but they didn't seem to feel anything. Nothing seemed to have any character, any style, you know. Everybody was helpful, everybody smiled and nodded, nobody seemed to be in a hurry, nobody seemed to be afraid of anything or fighting against anything, or moving toward anything. Who can live like that? Who would want to photograph that?"

"Life seemed a bit flat, huh?"

"Flat, yes. That's a good description. And speaking of flat, I walked around for two days looking for something to take pictures of, and couldn't find anything. Nothing. Well, there's scenery, but I don't do scenery. There are mountains in Montana, but they're a few hundred miles from Billings. In Billings, all you can see is sky and ground and short boring buildings. I guess living in the city has spoiled me. A snooty, entitled, East Coast twit. I hated Montana before I even got there, and I came home without one single picture."

"I probably would have come with you, you know. If you had asked me."

"Which is probably why I didn't ask. You would have hated it and pretty soon you would have hated me. You are built for the city even more than me."

We endured a long silence while she walked around the recliner and toyed with my bald spot. "We had a good run, Bird, but I don't feel like there's an 'us' anymore. Like I told you, you just don't need me."

"Then this was never really about Montana, was it? It was about us."

A slight, but honest, catch in her voice. "I don't know. Maybe that's true."

The room was silent, except for the chirp and whistle of Lancelot and Guinevere. They were both hanging on the bars of the cage, watching us intently, bird anthropologists trying to understand the curious behavior of these clumsy, wingless, lower life forms.

"What will you do now?" I asked.

She laughed a little...a nervous, guilty laugh. "I'm thinking of our last date at the park. You, clenched like a fist, and me singing, *"Old Friends."*

"Oh, yeah. Please don't tell me you heard it the other day and knew all the words."

"No, not all the words. But it did give me some ideas. I think I may have found a wonderful new subject to photograph. He's an elderly man, lives uptown. In fact, I may just photograph all the elderly people in that building."

"Aha. That's inspired. No more pears?"

"No, I think my pear period is over. Avant-garde has succumbed to realism. What about you?" She looked over at the court of new parquet tiles and the supports for the backboard. "What are you doing to the place now?"

"Basketball court. Larry Bird may have gone back to Indiana," I said, "but there will always be a part of him here in SoHo."

She picked up her dry cleaning and stepped into the elevator. "Do you think you'll ever finish the place?"

"I hope not," I said.

It took a little while, but after she was gone, I was finally able to think about her again. In the twentieth century, an age of stress, responsibility and relentless guilt, losing someone you love can be liberating. She was gone, so I couldn't fail her anymore. If she someday stopped caring about me, or even started hating me, at least I wouldn't know about it.

~ * ~

It took almost a month, but the book proved to be the real deal. Bernard Prowse's hunch had been right, and William Julian's evaluation confirmed the unimaginable. The handwriting belonged to Whitman, and the blood was found to be, almost certainly, Abraham Lincoln's. A genealogical study of Walter's family, done with the help of Marguerite, uncovered an ancestor named Henry who was a corporal in the Union army, and stationed in Washington at the time of the assassination.

"According to Mr. Julian," Paulie told me, "this Henry Rupert was probably a guard at Ford's Theatre and was stuck with the job of throwing away President Lincoln's bloody clothes. He came across the book purely by accident. He kept it, probably thinking it might come to be valuable. Or out of fear in the terrible aftermath of the assassination. Afterwards, he was afraid he would be branded a thief or a grave robber, and so he kept it hidden. He wouldn't even tell his family where it came from. They passed it from generation to generation on Henry's say-so that it was valuable." Paulie had said it weeks ago: it's a hard thing when you can't enjoy something you love.

"So you're a rich man now?" I asked.

He lifted his cup of low-fat eggnog to me and smiled. "In so many ways, Arthur. In so many ways."

~ * ~

I am writing this in late December, just after returning home from a Christmas party at Paulie's apartment. Marguerite Emerson, soon to revert to Marguerite Rupert, did most of the cooking, including five dozen gingerbread cookies. The place was bright and spotless and festive, just like I imagined it was in the days when Marguerite and her parents used to entertain Paulie. There was a new TV in the living room, new carpeting and drapes, and a whole new set of kitchen appliances. The furniture Walter had made was still there, polished and fragrant, connecting the past with the present, his heritage with the daily lives of those he left behind. There were photographs on the wall, too, not pear-shaped montages, but portraits of nobly weathered residents of this frontier landscape: Paulie smiling from a bench in

Central Park, Mrs. Federico and James looking nervous at her kitchen table, and Paulie and Marguerite on the steps outside the building, pointing and laughing at something beyond the camera.

So I sit here now with my feet on a windowsill, sipping tea and watching my small rectangle of the Hudson River. The days are short and the sun is far away. On the ledge of the building across the street, a half dozen pigeons squat, huddled together for warmth and companionship. Another swoops in to make a flapping landing on the narrow ledge and casually joins the group. Maybe that's the secret knowledge Paulie and I share. Smooth landings aren't always graceful, and even the edge of a long fall can be comfortable if you know how to keep your balance. Survivors need to find each other, rely on each other, and pull close together when the cold wind blows.

Meet Gene Murray

Gene is a retired special education professional living and writing in upstate New York. This is his second novel published by Wings ePress. Over a long life, he's been a smiling toddler, a reluctant student, a crossing guard, body surfer, and Mickey Mantle wannabe. He has a family, nuclear in more ways than one, that he cares for deeply and worries about in the traditional 'wee small hours of the morning.' They are the star around which his wobbly planet orbits.

Writing has become the activity that keeps him balanced in these unbalanced times.

Other Works From The Pen Of

Gene Murray

Mcguffin – Two fans at the Woodstock Festival witness an inexplicable event, and their lives are affected by it until they meet and investigate thirty years later.

Letter to Our Readers

Enjoy this book?

You can make a difference

As an independent publisher, Wings ePress, Inc. does not have the financial clout of the large New York Publishers. We can't afford large magazine spreads or subway posters to tell people about our quality books.

But, we do have something much more effective and powerful than ads. We have a large base of loyal readers.

Honest Reviews help bring the attention of new readers to our books.

If you enjoyed this book, we would appreciate it if you would spend a few minutes posting a review on the site where you purchased this book or on the Wings ePress, Inc. webpages at:

https://wingsepress.com/

Thank You

Visit Our Website

For The Full Inventory
Of Quality Books:

Wings ePress.Inc
https://wingsepress.com/

Quality trade paperbacks and downloads
in multiple formats,
in genres ranging from light romantic comedy
to general fiction and horror.
Wings has something for every reader's taste.
Visit the website, then bookmark it.
We add new titles each month!

Wings ePress Inc.
3000 N. Rock Road
Newton, KS 67114